Frank Barrett

The Admirable Lady Biddy Fane

Vol. I.: Her Surprising Curious Adventures in Strange Parts & Happy...

Frank Barrett

The Admirable Lady Biddy Fane
Vol. I.: Her Surprising Curious Adventures in Strange Parts & Happy...

ISBN/EAN: 9783337020927

Printed in Europe, USA, Canada, Australia, Japan

Cover: Foto ©Andreas Hilbeck / pixelio.de

More available books at **www.hansebooks.com**

THE ADMIRABLE LADY BIDDY FANE:

HER SURPRISING CURIOUS ADVENTURES IN
STRANGE PARTS & HAPPY DELIVERANCE
FROM *PIRATES, BATTLE, CAPTIVITY,* & OTHER
TERRORS ; WITH DIVERS *ROMANTIC & MOVING
ACCIDENTS* AS SET FORTH BY BENET
PENGILLY (HER COMPANION IN MISFOR-
TUNE & JOY), & NOW FIRST DONE INTO
PRINT

BY

FRANK BARRETT.

Author of "Folly Morrison," "Honest Davie," &c.

VOL. I.

CASSELL & COMPANY, LIMITED:

LONDON, PARIS, NEW YORK & MELBOURNE.

1888.

CONTENTS.

THE ADMIRABLE LADY

BIDDY FANE.

CHAPTER I.

I AM TAKEN OUT OF THE PILLORY AND NARROWLY ESCAPE GOING TO THE WHIPPING-POST.

As 'tis the present mode to embellish a history with a portrait of the writer, it will not be amiss if I here at the outset give you some hints by which you may see, as in a frontis-piece, the image of that Benet Pengilly who is about to tell you many marvellous things.

What kind of man I am you may better judge when you come to the last page of this history; my business now is to pre-sent my image as I was; to which end I would have you picture a man close upon

B

thirty years of age, clad in a jerkin and
breeches of leather, six foot and some odd
inches in height, gaunt and lean as a
famished wolf, fierce - visaged, with an un-
kempt beard of hair, and a shock ragged
as a bush, and both as black as any ink;
a deep - sunk, bloodshot eye, and a swarthy
skin, all besmirched with broken egg, filth,
and blood. This pretty portraiture you shall
frame in the town pillory, which stood over
against the Church of St. Mary, in the city
of Truro, with this very true description writ
under the headpiece ·—

"BENET PENGILLY, A STURDY ROGUE."

And now to begin my story, I must tell you
that I had stood in this pillory from sunrise,
a sport for all the cowards in the town. I
say cowards, for surely those who have courage
are never cruel to the helpless, and these—
the strongest of whom would have fled before
me had I been free—had baited me as curs
bait a tethered bull, without any kind of

mercy, jeering at me, and making me a mark for any beastliness that came to hand, ay, and sharp stones to boot, as the blood from my lips and cheek testified.

There were never less than a couple of score of this rabble about me, hallooing and whooping; for as fast as one left me to go about his business, another took his place. But amongst the constantly changing crowd was one who, seated upon the stone bench where the town porters are wont to rest their loads awhile, never took his eyes off me, nor budged from his place from the time he came hither, which was about ten o'clock, till now, when the sun was past the meridian. He watched me as a surgeon marks the bearing of his subject under the knife; nay, rather 'twas as a fiend might watch the torment of the damned, for a hellish smile crept over his face as some insult more cruel than the rest provoked me to a state of desperation.

This man I had seen before. His name was Rodrigues. 'Twas he who, in the month

B 2

of March, came into Plymouth, his ship all
decked out with ribbons, his crew arrayed in
lace and cambric, and every mother's son as
drunk as a beggar; 'twas he who had set
tubs of sherries on the Hoe, staved iu the
heads, and in sheer wantonness and drunken
folly cast the wine right and left with his
joined palms; to say nothing of divers other
senseless tricks whereby in something less than
two months he had squandered treasure to
the value of nigh upon £7,000, and left not
enough, when his ship was seized, to pay the
King's dues. He still wore the remnants and
wreck of his former finery—silk stockings, satin
trunks, velvet doublet, and a hat with a
feather in it; but, lord! so broken, stained,
and bedrabbled through his mad frolics that
plain homespun had looked rich beside it.

I have heard that this Rodrigues was of
gipsy origin, and indeed he looked fierce and
brutal enough for that or anything else. He
had a short, curling beard. His hair grew
low down on his brows, and fell behind his

ears in long, wiry ringlets. His eyes were
small, but remarkably piercing, and the aspect
of his face was very eager and cruel; but that
which made his looks most terrible was his
teeth, which were pointed sharp, like a wolf's,
so that when he displayed them he looked
more like a beast of prey than a natural man.
This peculiarity, however, was not due to his
birth, but was rather brought about, as I
learnt, through living many years a captive
amongst cannibal savages, whose practice it is
to file their teeth after this fashion. In addi-
tion to this disfigurement his ears were slit,
and he had a long white scar quartered down
his tawny cheek; in short, he was as ill-
looking and horrid a scoundrel as ever I did
see.

'Twas, as I say, high noon, and matters
stood thus, when, of a sudden, the clamour of
my persecutors was stilled as by enchantment,
and the sound of horse with the jingling of
harness struck on my ear; and, casting my eye
in that direction, I perceived a company of

ladies and gentlemen with their servants, all
very richly mounted, drawing hither. I took
not much heed of them to discern who they
were, being callous sick with the pain and insult I had suffered so many hours, until they
drew near within a stone's cast to see what
sport was forward, when Rodrigues, jumping
down from his stone bench, and making them
a mighty respectful obeisance of his battered
hat with its broken feather, my curiosity was
pricked, and I once more looked that way.
Then my heart sank lower than ever, and I
would have been thankful had my face been
beat out of all recognition ; for foremost among
the company was Lady Biddy Fane, and 'twas
clear by the anger in her face that she recognised me. Yet, the next moment was I glad,
and my heart was lifted up with a savage
exultation ; for now, thinks I, she will see to
what degradation and ruin hath she brought a
man of promise by her cruelty.

I do not think there ever was in the whole
world a young woman so beautiful as Lady

Biddy Fane; nor is there like to be again.
Had I not thought so, should I have abandoned myself to despair because of her cruelty?
Nay; nor should I have had this history to
tell. And yet may there be women as straight
and fairly proportioned as she, though none
more so; and others with a skin of that rare
pale clearness; and others, again, with eyes as
large and dark and spirited, with sweet lips
lined with snowy teeth, with a perfect nose
(shapely as any Greek's) and wavy, nut-brown
hair; still, I say, you shall not find another
one woman in whom are combined the graces
of so many together, with a spirit so lofty,
noble, fearless, and faithful as hers. I might
discourse of her beauty for many pages, and
yet fail, for want of words, to do her justice;
but to make an end of this matter briefly, I
say again she was incomparable.

On her right hand was my uncle, Sir
Bartlemy Pengilly, Knight, the same who ad-
ventured with Sir Walter Raleigh in the quest
for gold upon the Oronoque; and a hale, lusty

old man he was, very personable, with shining
white hair that curled closely over his head,
and a well-clipped beard; on her left hand
was Sir Harry Smidmore, a young man of good
parts, as I must acknowledge, albeit I hated
him exceedingly, by reason of his standing in
better. grace with Lady Biddy Fane than any
other of her suitors, and they were as numerous
as butterflies over a fair garden on a summer's
day. Besides these three were many friends
of theirs of very good condition; but they
enter not into this history, so enough is said
of them.

Now, the rabble, thinking this company
was drawn up for amusement, presently began
to make sport of me; and one caught up a
dead cat (which had served before) and flung
it at me, and another a cabbage stump,
which had likewise served; and a third, finding nothing handier than a broken pantile,
was about to cast that, when Sir Harry
Smidmore, with the flat of his sword, fetched
him a clap on the arm that made him think

better of it. Then Lady Biddy, with scorn
and disgust on her countenance, turned away,
and the whole company followed her thence,
whispering together, and all very grave; for
it was known that I was Sir Bartlemy's
nephew, and a kinsman of Lady Biddy's,
and that I had disgraced them before their
friends.

After them went Rodrigues also, at a
brisk pace to keep up with the horse. They
had not been gone long when there came
two of the sheriff's men with a cord to
loose me, whereupon seeing that I was about
to be taken from the pillory, the whole
rout that were in the square took to their
heels as though a tiger were about to be
let loose on them; for I was a man of terror
for many miles about, and was known as
" Ben of the Woods."

The sheriff's men first freed my hands
from the boards, and, making fast my arms
about me with their cord, they unlocked the
headpiece, and then, having given me a

draught from a pitcher, for I reeled like one in liquor being taken down, they led me up the High Street to the Dolphin Inn, and so into the great room there, where at a table sat the justice who had condemned me to the pillory, with Sir Bartlemy Pengilly, Sir Harry Smidmore, and some others; and against the wall in the shadow I spied Rodrigues.

Being brought to the end of the table facing this company, the justice made me a discourse, and the gist of his matter was that, out of respect for Sir Bartlemy, he had taken me from the pillory before my time, and would absolve me from further punishment if I would give my word to be of better conduct henceforth and agree to the proposal Sir Bartlemy was about to make.

Then Sir Bartlemy, pushing aside the bottle that stood before him, leaned forward and addressed me thus—

" Ben," says he, " I am heartily ashamed of you, and with the greater reason because you are not ashamed of yourself. Look at me, rogue! Do you see that my eyes are full of tears? 'Tis for shame that you are my nephew that I weep, and not for pity, for I do assure you, sir" (turning to the justice), "I loved this fellow, and not so long since, neither; a brave - looking and comely man he was but a year ago; of good parts and great promise, whom I had been proud to call my son; and a brave man he should be by reason that his father endured manfully much hardship in adventuring under Sir Francis Drake, and died beside Sir Richard Grenville fighting those fifteen great gallions of the Spaniard. But what a base, desperate rascal are you" (turning again to me in anger) "to abandon yourself to despair, to yield up everything without a struggle and at the first shot of adversity, bringing dishonour upon your family thus! Had you but yourself to think of, vagabond? Had your father thought only of his own comfort, would he willingly have

endured hardship and privation, or sought to
face the Spanish guns? 'Twas the honour
and glory of his queen he thought of before
all; and had you truly loved your cousin,
you would have set up her happiness before
your own, and done naught to make her
blush for so base a subject."

"Ay, surely!" cries the justice, frowning
upon me.

" Yet must we not be too hard on the fellow,
neither," says Sir Bartlemy, turning again to
him; "for 'tis not as if he had forsaken a
life of pain for one of pleasure, but quite the
contrary; for he was light-hearted and gay
before this cruel stroke; and now what creature
on the face of this smiling world is more deplorable? And, truly, for a man to abandon
himself to a life of such desolation and misery
as he passes in the woods, his mind must be
unstrung, and all its music turned to discord;
and there is naught, I hear, like disappointment in love to unsettle the reason, though
nothing of the sort has ever troubled mine;

for if one lass frowned I'd quickly find another
who'd smile; and I warrant," says he, merrily,
with a sly dig at the stout old justice—" I
warrant you have often done the same, Master
Anthony."

"Let us go to the point, Sir Bartlemy—to
the point," said the justice, severely.

"That will I with no more ado. Look
you, rascal," says my uncle, thumping the table
and bending his brows on me, "you have done
little that I should love you, and much to
undo the love I bore you; yet will I make an
effort to save you from disgrace for your
father's sake—and something for your own—
for, God knows, you are a wretch as much
to be pitied as hated; so here to the point.
I am bent upon getting that treasure which
lies, as we know full well, beyond the Oronoque, in order that it fall not into the hands
of the Spaniard. 'Tis too late for me to
make this venture under my own command,
though I fain would; but a worthy commander
have I found, and under him you shall take

service as his lieutenant and second in command, and share the profits of this enterprise
in due proportion.

"Wait!" cries the justice; "here surely is
a mistake! You cannot intend to place this
fellow taken from the pillory next in position
to your commander!"

"He is my brother's son," replies Sir
Bartlemy, "and I have faith that he will bear
himself well when this present distemper of
mind shall be blown off by the wholesome
sea gales; for the rest, this matter concerns
the crew of the ship and the commander. If
they are willing, should I object?"

"But are they willing?" asks the justice.
"There is the point."

"Here is the ablest man of the crew—one
who has sailed with Drake, gone through
many perilous adventures, and been himself
a master. Hear what he says. Speak up,
Rodrigues."

Rodrigues came out of the shadow, and,
pointing his finger at me, says he—"That man

is worth any ten men of our crew, and such a man a crew needs for master. We want no puppets, but men who can fight and suffer with stiff lips." Then he dropped back into the shadow again.

I was grateful to this man. Hope—that so long had lain dead within me—sprang up to life, and an eager desire for wild adventure seized upon me. And at that moment the door at the end of the room over against the head of the table opened, and Lady Biddy Fane came into the room; then my imagination, already kindled, blazed up with a mad conception of winning untold gold, glory, and honour—all to lay at her feet, with the possibility that she might accept them and me.

But, lord! there was little in her aspect to encourage such a hope, as she stood there erect and scornful, her pretty brows bent in angry scorn as she looked on me, tapping her silk skirt impatiently with her riding-whip. But this did not daunt my spirit, for I knew how sweet those brows were when they unbent, and that her dainty hand was more apt to caress than to strike.

While my heart was aflame with this sudden return of passion, the justice spoke—

"What says the commander? There the point is, I take it."

"Speak up, Sir Harry," says Sir Bartlemy.

"I will have him for my lieutenant as willingly as I would make him my friend," says Sir Harry Smidmore.

Hearing this my heart being filled with jealousy rebelled against my reason, for I knew not until that moment who was to be the commander of this expedition.

"Now, Ben," says Sir Bartlemy, "you have the chance to redeem the past—ay, more than that—to make us love you as we never loved you yet. Will you accept the offer freely made by us?"

"What!" says I to myself, "win gold and honours for Smidmore to lay at her feet? Never!" And so I laughed with a brutal scorn and shook my head.

"An obstinate, contumacious rascal," cries Sir Bartlemy, with one of those sea oaths which he was more free to utter than I have been to set down here; "yet," says he, softening in a moment, "must we bear with him by reason of his misfortunes to the utmost limits. I have failed; plead thou for him, dear girl" (turning to Lady Biddy), "or he must go back again to the pillory."

"Ay, with all my heart," says Lady Biddy, advancing; "and, as you love me, sir," bending slightly to the justice, "I do beg you to favour my pleading. Send him not back to the pillory, for sure when that, together with my uncle's gentle, kind persuasion, fails to win him to a decent behaviour, 'tis evident that a sharper remedy is needed for his disorder. Prythee, then, dear sir, send him to the whipping-post; there to be soundly whipped."

"Why, so I will," cries the justice, cheerfully, clapping his fist on the table; "for I've heard no better suggestion this bout. To the whipping-post he shall go."

c

· " Not alive," I muttered ; and then straining with all my might I burst the cords that
bound me, and turned to the door; whereupon
the sheriff's men threw themselves before me.
But one I took by the throat and the other
by the shoulder, and swinging them together
I flung them against the wall with such force
that the oak panels cracked again, and they
sank to the ground like things of clay.   Then
I strode out of the room and thence into the
pure air, and no one had the stomach to
stay me.

CHAPTER II.

SIR BARTLEMY's house was built upon a hill
not far from St. Maw's, and looked over Falmouth Haven to Penny-come-quick. His
estate was mostly woodlands, and skirting the
river Fal extended north beyond Philligh and
east as far as Tregony. In the midst of these
woods had I lived for many months unmo-
lested, the worthy old knight, with good intent, bidding his foresters let me kill what
game I would for my use; and here had I
built me a hut as a shelter against the in-
clemency of the weather, thatching it with
broom and sods of turf. But 'twas a mistaken
kindness on his part, for this sufferance only
tended to complete that state of savagery into
which I was sinking.

c 2

From childhood I have loved the woods,
and found delight in studying the secrets of
nature—the growth of herbs, the places where
they may be found; the ways of birds and
beasts, and the like; and when my hopes were
all cast over, I had fled thither, saying, "Here
is a mistress whose smile is not to be wooed
in vain!" And, indeed, for a troubled spirit
I know no comfort so soothing as the woods
after a spring shower, when all is fresh and
sweet, and every little blade of grass seems to
smile. For the most part my state was that
of utter solitude. Many a day I heard no
sound but my own footfall, and saw nothing
but the still trees. For weeks and weeks I
met no human creature; yet had I no inclination to seek a companion. But at times my
nature would revolt against this unnatural condition of solitude, and a mad thirst for de-
bauchery would seize me. Then with my bow
would I kill a buck, and, selling it to those
who were ever ready to buy venison of me at
a fourth of its value, I would go into Truro

and spend my money in some gross frolic like that which had brought me to the pillory (as I have shown).

And now, having dwelt long enough on my originals, yet not too long, for I would show truly to what degradation may a man bring himself by self-abandonment, I will continue this history without any further digression.

To my hut, then, in the wood did I betake myself after my escape from Truro, refreshing myself on the way with a plunge in the cool river; and being arrived at my home, as I may call it, I went to a hollow tree hard by, which served me as a storehouse, to see if aught was there to satisfy the cravings of my stomach; but finding nothing save a hare which I had hung there before leaving, and which now stank (for I had been absent best part of three days) so that I could not eat it, hungered though I was, I picked up my bow, which also I kept in this place, and, taking a turn in the wood,

I had presently the chance to kill a wood-pigeon. Then I built a fire with dry sticks, of which there was no lack at this season, laid my pigeon in the embers, and when it had lain there as long as my patience would endure, I stripped off the skin and feathers, and devoured it, using my fingers for fork and my teeth for knife; and thus having partly quieted my stomach, though I could have eaten half a dozen such small game, but was too tired to seek more, I threw myself on the earth within my hut, and fell asleep at once, nor did any pricking of conscience trouble me in the least.

And here I slept on till about eight o'clock in the evening, as I judge, when an unwonted sound awoke me ; for I had contracted the habit of sleeping, as it were, with my ears open. But being mighty heavy with sleep I did no more than sit up and glance stupidly through the opening of my hut. I saw naught but a tranquil glow over the west through the still leaves of the trees ; and a nightingale then bursting out into song at no great distance, I concluded there was nothing to fear; and throwing myself on the ground, in a minute I was again sound asleep.

Nothing disturbed me after that through the night, but soon after daybreak, as I take it, my ears were assailed by a confusion of sounds, and ere I could spring to my feet, a fellow threw himself upon my chest, another knelt upon my legs, and a third laid strong hands upon my shoulders, and in a trice I felt cords cutting into my arms and binding them to my sides.

" You escape not this time, Master Benet," growled a voice, and in truth my captors were as good as this fellow's words, for enough cord was bestowed about me as would have trussed up an elephant. My captors were six ; all stout fellows and well armed, amongst whom I recognised one of the men who had served me the day before, and I cursed my folly that I had lain myself open

to be taken in this way; for I might have
foreseen the pursuit had I given it a thought.
However, cursing was of no good; there was
I clapped up and in a fair way to get my
punishment doubled, and more than that.
And, as there was no likelihood of escape,
the only thing left me was to bear my ill-
luck with the fortitude of despair. Yet my
heart sank as I saw them take up my bow
which. I had laid beside me on going to
sleep, for I knew I should have it no more,
and how could I get food or aught else without that when I got my liberty again?
Better to take my life, or rob me for ever
of my liberty, than take that by which I
lived, thought I.

They haled me out into the open, and
there for the first time this day I spied the
gipsy Rodrigues. He was seated on a fallen
tree, with his elbows on his knees, and his
jaws in his hands, smoking tobacco in the end
of a clay pipe; and now he had his keen eyes
fixed on me, watching how I took this new

buffet of fortune with the same look he had worn the day before, when I stood in the pillory.

I guessed it was his step that had aroused me the foregoing evening, and that he led on the sheriff's men to catch me, which was pretty near the truth of the matter, as I shall presently show.

To make sure that I should not escape, the men tied me up to a tree; then they proceeded to regale themselves from a store of meat, with which their wallets were well filled, making very merry with me the time; after which they consulted together in a low voice; and, one of them having parleyed for a few minutes with Rodrigues, they all stretched themselves out on the soft sward, and in a short time were asleep and snoring like so many swine, which surprised me somewhat, seeing that now the sun was getting pretty high.

For some while Rodrigues sat as still as any carved image, smoking his pipe and looking

at me; then up he gets, and passing the
sleepers as silently as might be, he comes to
my side; and putting first his finger on his
lips, and jerking his thumb over his shoulders
with a sly leer to bid me be silent, he pulls
a letter from his breast and showed me my
name writ upon it. This he thrusts back
in his breast, and, after a glance over his
shoulder to make sure all were still sleeping,
he cuts the cords that bound me to the tree
with his dagger, and leads me a good stonecast
distant, where we might converse in a low tone
without being heard.

Here he again lugged out the letter, and,
spreading it out (the seal being already broke),
he held it before my eyes to read; for he had
been careful not to sever the cords that tethered
my arms to my side.

It was my uncle's hand and signature.

"You have read this?" says I.

Rodrigues shrugged his shoulders, as much
as to say, "I had been a fool else," and then
says he, with the utmost assurance—

"I was to have given it to you last night, but you were sleeping so sweetly I had no heart to wake you. Besides, I thought you would more readily listen to his advice if you were in bonds than if you were free."

"So you betrayed me?"

"Not at once. I led the fellows up and down in the moonlight best part of the night, that they might be overcome with fatigue this morning, and so give me the opportunity of some serious conversation with you. Now read what Sir Bartlemy has to say."

I was in no position to resent this insolence; so I did what was next best—swallowed it, and followed his advice; and this is what I read:—

"NEPHEW BENET,—You are no longer safe in my woods, for I have no power to shield you from the law. Even now the officers are out to apprehend you, and God knows what may befall if you are taken. If you have any feeling for me, any love for your father's memory, or any respect for yourself, you will escape this new shame. My ships lie in the haven ready to depart, and Sir Harry is still willing to accept you as his companion

and friend in the noble enterprise now toward. I do
beg and implore you be not a fool and a villain as
well, but quickly accept this offer. Rodrigues, who bears
this, does undertake to carry you safe to Flushing, where
a boat lies in readiness to take you on board the *Sure
Hawk*, where you shall find all comfort and good cheer
to say naught of the loving gratitude of thine old uncle,   ˙

"BARTLEMY PENGILLY."

This gentle letter did somewhat move my
heart; and surely its sensibility had been
gone beyond all recovery had it not responded
to so warm an appeal; and my first feeling
was that I would do his bidding. Then I
bethought me what a mean and sneaking
thing it was, after refusing this offer when I
was free to accept it when I was not free; and
what a hang-dog cur I should appear to all
the crew when my story became known, and
how (under the mask of pity and patronage)
Sir Harry Smidmore must scorn me for a
paltry fellow. And with that came the re-
membrance of Lady Biddy's contempt; and,
coupling these two together, I was wrought
again with fierce jealousy and hatred; and I

did resolve that I would die ten thousand deaths rather than give them this food for their scorn.

Rodrigues, subtly watching me, must have seen the madness in my eye, for he whispered at this point—

" Sir Harry is wondrous eager to get you."

" Curse Sir Harry ! " says I, warmly.

" Not I," says he, with a quiet laugh. " He'll give me a score of gold pieces if I take you to him ; and no wonder, for he will be well repaid with caresses when he takes the news to Lady Biddy."

" You'll get no pieces from him, nor he kisses from her, through me, I promise you."

" Your ears will be cropped for a certainty if you are taken back to Truro." And then, as I made no reply, he adds, " You are minded to break your uncle's heart rather than your own pride."

" Nay," says I, " there's a way by which I may spare him shame, and myself as well."

"Are you man enough to thrust a knife
in your own heart?" says he.

"Ay!" says I, joyfully; "do but try me.
Give but my forearm fair play and lend me
your dagger. You shall be rewarded, I warrant,
when you tell Lady Biddy I am no more. Or
do you thrust it into me if you doubt the use
I should make of the knife. I promise you I
will not awake a single sleeper with my groans."

He nodded approvingly, but made no
attempt to take me at my word.

"Life isn't worth much," says he, "to a
fool. And 'tis only a fool who thinks there's
never another loaf to be got when he's eaten
his last crust. Look at me," spreading his
arms and surveying his rags—"a prince last
month, a beggar to-day. What of that? I'll
be a king next year. And so may you be,"
he adds, after a pause. But that did not
tempt me; so presently he goes on—

"If you had seen what I have seen, and
if you were as hideous as I am, and as old,
yet you would not talk of ending your life.

If you had seen as I have seen "—speaking slowly, yet with passion, as, through his half-closed eyes, he seemed to be looking at what he described—" a land where the forests are flower gardens, more fair than hand of man can make; where trees—not like these stunted things, which are but bushes by comparison—where trees, I say, seem hung with precious gems, and waters run on beds of gold and silver, and every rock is dazzling crystal; where rich fruits tempt the appetite they never cloy; where flying birds are like the flash of gems, and their song more sweet than your musician ever heard in dreams; where the sun never parches nor cold winds bite; where the gentle air is brisk as wine and charged with the scent of leagues of flowers: if you had seen that land, I say, you would want to see it again before you died."

These hints of southern glories I had heard before from my uncle; though between his speech and this poetic gipsy's there was all the difference betwixt north and south.

"To see this land might tempt you to
oblige Sir Bartlemy," says he. Then, after a
bit, he continues, "But it does not, I perceive.
You know the intent of this enterprise—first,
to gratify your uncle's whim ; and, next, to enrich Sir Harry, that he may wed Lady Biddy.
You have no relish to help him that way—
to come home with a gruesome face to pull
the joybells at their wedding ? "

"No, by the lord ; that will I never do ! "
says I.

" Then your answer to that letter is
' No ? ' "

"A thousand times ' No ! ' "

" You refuse the offer ? "

" I do."

" I see you mean what you say," says he,
looking me keenly in the eye, " and I am
right glad it is so. I am not mistaken in
you, Pengilly. I saw there was mettle in
you from the first, else I had not taken all
this trouble on myself to win you. Had you
said ' Yes ' to that letter you would have had

me for your enemy, and it would have gone ill with you, I promise. As it is, I am your friend, as I will quickly prove. For, first, I will give you freedom, and after that a voyage to the south; whence you shall speedily return, your ship deep laden with gold: then shall you have possession of your mistress. All this I promise; ay, and more, for you shall, if you will, revenge yourself of the insults this proud maid has heaped upon you, and humble the man who would have taken her from you, so that he shall not dare to show his face before her. What say you to this?"

I could say nothing on the moment, being greatly perplexed by this unexpected turn; and ere I could command my senses to inquire of Rodrigues how he purposed compassing that which he proposed, we were both mightily startled by hearing, at no great distance behind us, the sound of men's voices; and presently one above the rest set to hallooing "Jack Geddes! Jack Geddes!" which was the name

D

of that sheriff's man who had bound me as aforesaid. Then on the other side we heard the men who lay asleep rousing each other with a great confusion of sound that showed they had discovered my escape. Thus we stood between the party which had taken me and a second party sent after to help them. And the chance of getting freedom, to say nothing of riches and my sweetheart, looked more unlikely than ever. Yet did we contrive to escape, as I shall set forth in the next chapter.

CHAPTER III.

THE two parties of sheriff's men were distant
from each other, as I took it by the sound of
their voices, no more than a hundred yards, so
that we could not burst away in any direction
without hazard of being seen; and a foolhardy
hazard it had been, for Jack Geddes and his
party were armed with muskets, and would
not have scrupled to use them. Yet how to
escape did not appear until Rodrigues (as luck
would have it) spied a fairly deep hole which
had served at one time for a sawpit, and to
this he hurried me, and we both leaped in,
and there, in a twinkling, did he scrape aside
the loose sawdust that lay at the bottom;
and in the trough thus hastily made, I, seeing

D 2

his intent, threw myself full length, and as
quickly was smothered over from top to toe
with the sawdust, so that nothing was visible
of me.

By this time the two parties were joined,
and there they set up a great shouting and
cursing because I was no longer bound to the
tree as I had been left. And not only did
they curse me, but they cursed Rodrigues as
heartily, vowing they would pepper him with
their bullets as a faithless villain if they saw
him. Whereupon this Rodrigues, laying himself prone on my body, set up a most dismal
groaning, like one in pain, hearing which
Jack Geddes and the rest came rushing to the
edge of the pit. Seeing him there all alone
and doubled up as though he had been broke,
half a dozen, in one breath, began to question
him how he came there, what was amiss with
him, etc. To which he replies with a groan—

" 'Tis all along of that Pengilly! I was but
dozing, when I heard one cry ' Jack Geddes ' "
(here a groan), "and the same moment I

saw Pengilly with a mighty wrench tear himself from the tree.   Up I started and after him, when, being but half awake, I threw myself into this cursed hole, and here have I broke my arm, I do believe.   But do you leave me here (where I am as well as elsewhere), and catch the villain.   I would not for the loss of both arms miss seeing his ears cropped."

"Ay! we will catch him: have no fear," says Geddes; "scatter yourselves, my fine fellows, and shoot down the rascal if you do but sight him, for we shall suffer for it if he escape us."

Whereupon the men, more concerned for themselves than for any hurt of Rodrigues, started off like hounds unleashed, and each, in his several direction, bent upon taking me again alive or dead.   And it was none too soon, for the sawdust, entering my mouth and nostrils when I breathed, I was pretty nigh choked—to say nothing of the oppression I suffered from the cords that pinned my arms and Rodrigues lying upon my back.

So when they were gone and Rodrigues, standing up and peering over the edge, said that all was clear, I lifted my head, shaking off the sawdust and spitting out that which had got into my throat, and breathed again.

"Now," said Rodrigues; "now may we escape, for being all scattered, our pursuers are less likely to take us."

"Do but cut this cord," says I, "and I warrant not any two shall take me."

"Ay," says he, "I will cut your bonds with a good heart. But first must you swear to be secret and silent; nay, you must swear also to be obedient to my direction without question or murmuring, else will I leave you here to fare for yourself."

I promised him this, for I was in no position to haggle over terms; yet my promise was not enough for him, but he, taking his dagger by the blade, held it to my mouth, and would have me kiss the cross of it, swearing by that sign as a Christian to obey him in every particular. And this I did, the

more readily because of the cord which Jack
Geddes had knotted so cruelly about my arms
that it bit into my flesh to my intolerable
hurt.

Having thus made me take oath, he cut the
cord, and I was free ; yet for some time could I
not use my arms with any freedom, by reason
they were so benumbed and bruised.   Nevertheless, I managed to scramble up out of the
pit after Rodrigues, and thence, I following
on his heels, with the stealth of any cats, we
pushed our way by bush and briar through the
thickest part of the wood, where, at sight of
an enemy, we might lie down and be unseen.
On we went, Rodrigues leading and keeping
the sun well before, for a matter of three miles
or thereabouts, without encountering any of my
pursuers ; and then, perceiving that if we kept
on in this direction we must shortly come to
Flushing, which lies (as I have said) on the
hither side of the Fal, opposite Penny-come-
quick, I twitched Rodrigues by the skirt and
gave him to understand this, adding that there

was not a fisherman there but knew me, and
would have me hanged if he could; and this
was true, for I was known and feared all round
and about these parts, and held to be a wild man
of the woods, very dreadful and dangerous, and
a bogey to frighten children withal.

"I know well enough where I am going,"
says he.

"That may be," says I; "yet this is but
a stepping out of the frying-pan into the fire,
so far as I am concerned."

Whereupon he taps the handle of his dagger
as a sign to me to remember my oath, and that
is all the satisfaction I got.

So on we go again, still keeping the sun
before us; and descending the hill anon we
come to the river side, and here Rodrigues
stops, looking to the right and left, as if uncer-
tain; then, putting his hand over his mouth,
he gives the cry of "Cuckoo!" as natural as
ever I did hear, and straight there comes an
answer in the same manner from a thicket
further up the river side. Thither we made

our way, but with great care, now being no more than a furlong or thereabouts from the village, screened off by a jutting point of land well timbered; and soon, passing through the said thicket, we came on a little creek, in which lay a boat, wherein sat a couple of seamen as tawny as Rodrigues, but stouter and better favoured, albeit one lacked an eye.

All about this creek there lay an open space, from which an alley ran up into the wood; and, lest he should be observed, Rodrigues would not advance beyond the brush, whence he signalled his fellows to know if all were safe. And he with the one eye, rising up and stretching himself as if he were aweary, spied up the alley and all round and about, and then signalled, by winking his one eye, that he could see nothing; whereupon Rodrigues bade me cross the open quickly, get into the boat, and lie down under the sail that was there. He came not himself, but was gone when I got to the boat and cast my eye round for him. And here I may tell what I afterwards learnt concerning him. He made

his way back with all speed to the sawpit, and
lay there as if he had never budged when
the men came back from their search after
me, still feigning to be greatly hurt with his
arm, though happily assured that it was not
broken.

Meanwhile I, following his direction without
knowing what the end thereof might be, got
into the boat, and, lying down in the bottom,
was covered over with the sail-cloth by one of
the mariners, while the other loosed the boat
from its moorings ; and this was done none too
quickly, for as the fellow was stepping into the
boat from untying of the headline, who should
come down into the open but John Geddes himself, as I knew full well by his voice.

"Hold, there!" says he, hailing the seamen.
"Have you seen a great, sturdy fellow in a
leather jerkin pass this way?"

"Not we," replies one ; "and we've been on
the look-out for such a man since yesterday
afternoon—and a pox to him!"

"And, pray, who set you to wait for him?"

asked Geddes, and his voice told that he was now close by the boat's side.

"Why, that's my master's business that sent us, and none of yours," said the fellow.

"Hold your clapper, Ned, and lend a hand with your oar," cries his mate, "for the boat is aground, and I can't shove her off. Yo, ho! all together! yo, ho!—there we be! Now off we go, Pengilly or no Pengilly, for, curse me," says he, "my in'ards will stand this griping of hunger no longer."

Then there sprang up a dissension between the two seamen and Geddes, who would have them ferry him over to Penny-come-quick, and they would not; and he, laying the stock of his musket on the gunwale to draw the boat so that he might step in, one of them flung it off, while the other fetched him a blow on the head with his oar that laid Master Geddes senseless on his back. Then says the first to the other—

"Lay to, Ned, for God's sake, or mischief will come of this."

All this while I lay still under the sail-cloth, expecting, for the most part, nothing less but to feel Geddes his foot step on to me. But his business being so concluded, I heard nothing more but the dip of the oars, the ripple of water under me, and the working of the rowlocks, until one of the men says to the other, "Pull under her lee, that we be not seen from the shore;" and the next minute the boat bumped, and the sail-cloth being whipped off, I found that we lay under the side of a fine, high ship.

"Up you go, comrade, quick," says Ned (he with the one eye).

Then up the rope steps that hung by the ship's side I sped, and being come on deck was as speedily hustled down into the dark hold below, where they who had followed me down barricadoed me round about with divers barrels, bidding me lie quiet until I should be told it was safe to venture forth.

And all this time I knew not that I had come as a runaway aboard my uncle's ship the *Sure Hawk;* but so it was.

CHAPTER IV.

I COME TO THE CANARIES IN BETTER PLIGHT
THAN I STARTED.

WHEN the seamen had hidden me away, so that no man not knowing the ways of the ship could well come at me save by discharging the hold of its stores, one brought me some meat and drink, and then I was left to myself in the dark. For some time all was quiet above, but about noon, as I judge, I heard a great bustle on the decks of pulling ropes and the like, and this continued all day until the evening, when the anchors were drawn up and the ship made sail. And the reason of this commotion was that Rodrigues, having got away from the sheriff's men, under pretence of seeking relief for his arm, sped him to Sir Bartlemy Pengilly to tell him how I had refused his offer, but had nevertheless gone aboard the *Sure*

Hawk to escape the law; whereupon the knight,
mightily pleased with this turn, ordered Sir
Harry Smidmore, who then lay at his house,
to lose no time in departing, but to take advantage of the breeze now springing up to set
sail as soon as might be; and the stores being
all aboard and the crew in readiness, Sir Harry
set about this business at once. When the
men stood at the anchor ready to heave away,
Sir Bartlemy and Lady Biddy took an affec-
tionate farewell of Sir Harry, and bidding him
with tears God speed and a happy return,
quitted the ship. And so about eight o'clock
that evening the *Sure Hawk* (with her companion, the *Adventurer*) sailed out of Falmouth
Haven with me, Benet Pengilly, in the hold.

When we were fairly out to sea, Rodrigues
came down to me with another fellow bearing
a lantern, and bade me come out, and I was
not sorry; for besides that it was extremely
stuffy down there, so that there was no breathing with any comfort, the ship had begun to
roll and pitch in such a manner that I feared

every moment nothing less but to be crushed
by some chest or barrel being thrown upon
me, though, indeed, there was naught to fear
in that respect, as I learnt when I became
better acquainted with the manner of these
things. But, indeed, the sea ran unconscionably
high, and the ship laboured painfully all that
night and the next day, and after that the
next night again was no better, so that it was
surprising to me that we had not foundered.
Yet that was the last thing I feared, for, being
miserably ill and as sick as any dog, I do truly
think that had the ship split I should have
made no effort to save myself.

I had been stowed away between decks
amongst some bales of goods packed securely
in the fore part of the vessel, and here I lay,
with no comfort but a stone jar of water,
until, waking from a sound sleep, it might be
about noon and we now at sea three days,
I perceived that the storm had greatly abated,
and that my stomach was no longer qualmish,
but quickened with a huge hunger—as well

it might be after my long fast, etc. Then,
feeling brisker than I had yet felt since we
set sail, I sat up, and a savoury smell sharpen-
ing my appetite, I got upon my legs, and so
spied half a dozen seamen seated on chests
under the light of the hatchway before a
smoking mess of pork and pease. Thither I
made my way, though not without difficulty,
the ship still rolling immoderately, and begged
civilly that they would let me eat with them.
Whereupon one shoved the victuals towards
me that I might help myself, but not a word,
good or bad, did any of them speak, which
was more noticeable because they had all been
laughing and talking till they saw me. Presently a pipe sounded, and they all went up
above; then down comes Rodrigues, and it
was the first time I had seen him since we
were at sea. He had on his sea skirt and
large boots all running with water, for it still
was exceedingly foul weather, and his hat
tied down about his ears with a red kerchief.
But he was in good spirits, and asked me

cheerfully how I did as he seated himself
beside me and helped himself to meat; and
having answered his inquiry, I told him how
the seamen scowled at me, and begged to
know if I had done aught to deserve this in-
civility.

"Why, yes," says he; "for had it not been
to save you from the catchpoles, we should
never have ventured to sea in such a rising
gale. We have had no rest since we left
Falmouth, and like at any moment to have
gone to the bottom. For aught we know, our
consort is lost, and all hands with her, not
having been seen these two days. And this
is a great loss, besides being a bad beginning
to our enterprise, and all is set down to your
charge. However, it is in your power to make
them amends and win their love, and I make
no doubt you will."

"With all my heart," says I, "if you do
but show me how."

"All in good time," says he, tearing with
his pointed teeth the flesh off a knuckle-bone

E

of pork that he held in his hands; "all in good time. We can do nothing yet, but I look to you for help by-and-by, else had I not run all this risk for you. And yet," continues he, after a pause, flinging the knuckle-bone behind him—"yet it might be well for you to make friends with the captain at once. He asked to see you this morning."

"And who is this captain?" I asked, my curiosity awakening.

"Why, Sir Harry Smidmore, to be sure. Did I not tell you?"

"No," says I, moodily.

"Then you might have guessed it."

And this was true, if I had been in a humour for guessing.

"I have been trapped and despatched to sea to please Lady Biddy," says I, savagely.

"Well, you'll bear me no grudge for that. There was no way to save you but by getting you aboard the ship." Then, glancing round to see we were alone, he adds, dropping his voice, "And if Sir Harry Smidmore made to sea with you before you could escape, that he might please his sweetheart and keep you and her well asunder, 'twas no fault of mine neither. Don't you like it, Pengilly?"

I ground my teeth for response.

"Would you be even with him for this trick?" he asked, in the same low tone, and with a sinister leer.

"Ay, that I would!" says I.

"So would I in your place," says he. "If a man served me that way, I'd——"

Here he stopped, and taking up a jack-knife, he stuck it in the deal board that served as a bench, and pressed on it till the blade came out on the other side, and while he did this his sinewy hand grasped the board as if it were a throat, and his lips were drawn back close on his pointed teeth; then he looked sidelong at me, saying never a word, as if to know how I took this hint.

"I am no murderer," says I, terrified by his manner as much as by his suggestion.

"Why, who said you were?" says he,

E 2

with great show of indignation. "Cannot a
man by steady endeavour go through a difficulty as I have gone through that board with
this knife without doing a mischief? What
a fool should I be to counsel you to such an
end when our true success depends upon you
being good friends with our captain. Nay,"
he adds, "if I thought you would curb your
spirit to it, I would beg you to take Sir
Harry's hand, when he offers it to you, and
accept his friendship."

"That can I never do."

"So I thought. Howsomever, you must
do him no injury or insult at this present.
And, harkye, I know it for a fact that he
wants to give into your hand a sum of money
entrusted to him by your uncle for your particular use, that you might furnish yourself
presently with an equipment worthy of his
nephew ; and this you must not refuse to
take. Laugh as scornfully as you will, but
you must take it, and I will tell you for
why. When we get to a port, you will have

to make the crew merry in return for the hardships they have suffered on your account. You must win them to your side, for we can do nothing else."

"They shall have every penny I get, and welcome. But tell me what you mean when you say we can do nothing without having the men on our side?"

"I mean," says he, "that without them you will get neither riches nor your sweetheart."

"And how, having them, am I to win these ends?"

"Leave that to me. I have promised the achievement, and if you do but work patiently upon my instructions, I will not fall short of my word. More than this I cannot now tell you, but you shall know more hereafter. For the present, you can do nothing but win the affection of the men, and the captain also."

All this was a great mystery to me, and I could nohow fathom to the bottom of it; this only was clear, that I must follow Rodrigues'

bidding, not only because I was bound to
do so in a certain measure by reason of my
oath, but also because it was good policy.
So when I had refreshed myself by sousing
my head in a bucket of water, I went above,
and, holding on by the bulwarks, was much
amazed with the sight of the heaving seas,
which I had never before seen as now, all
around me, and the way in which the great
ship would dive down into the hollow of a
wave as if to perdition, and yet the next
moment ride upon the crest of it as light as
any duck.

While I was standing here, one of the seamen came to me, saying that the captain would
speak with me; so I went with him into the
roundhouse under the poop deck where Sir
Harry was, and very cheerful and bright this
young man looked in his sea dress.   Then,
with a noble, easy air, he begs me to sit down,
and, sitting himself, discoursed about the late
storm, telling me how we should certainly have
been all lost but for the admirable skill and

exertions of the master, Rodrigues (and this
every one did allow), and all with perfect self-
command and natural civility, as though we
had been the best friends in the world. But
he did not offer me his hand to take, and I
was glad of this, for I could not have taken
it without shame, feeling as I still did towards
him.

"However," says he, "the worst is over,
and, please God, the first part of our voyage
will soon be made; then you will be free to
do as you like—either to go back to England
or to go on with me. For I have not the
power to hold you a prisoner, nor have I the
wish to keep you with me, except as a friend.
That is for you to decide, and I hope, with
all my heart, you will decide to share in this
enterprise, and return with me a richer and a
happier man than ever you could have been
had you not sailed with us. And that your
choice may be perfectly free, here is a purse
of money that Sir Bartlemy entrusted me with
for your use. It will pay your voyage home,

but if you have need of more for your neces-
sities, I shall be very happy to place my purse
at your disposal."

I took the bag of money he offered, thank-
ing him for his civility as well as my untutored
tongue would allow. Then he rose, making me
a graceful bow, and bade the man who waited
at the door to take me to my cabin, which I
found very neat and properly furnished, with
everything necessary to my convenience, and
two good suits of new clothes, besides shirts,
stockings, etc.

Rodrigues was mightily pleased when he
saw me in my new clothes and with my hair
decently combed, and it seemed to me that the
seamen eyed me with more respect than they
had yet shown me ; indeed, I found that this
decency did elevate me in my own opinion a
great deal, so that I thought better of myself
and more hopefully than I had since the beginning of my misfortunes.

The wind continued very high (but fairly
prosperous) for nine days after that, and then,

making the Canaries, we came into water as smooth as the heart of man could desire, and so cast anchor at Fuerteventura. And here we were very busy for three days, repairing the mischief done us by the storm, and all that time we saw nothing of the *Adventurer*, our consort, which was to have joined us there in case of being separated, so that we gave her up for lost, and I know not who was more cast down about this, Sir Harry Smidmore or Rodrigues. However, on the fourth day the missing ship bore in sight (to our great joy), and by nightfall was anchored alongside of us, but with one mast gone, and so sorely bruised that she looked not the same ship she had been. And it was curious to see how the crew of the *Adventurer*, coming on board the *Sure Hawk*, the men did hug each other and weep for gladness. Amongst them all the most joyful were Rodrigues and Ned Parsons, the seaman I have spoken of as having only one eye, and who was master aboard the *Adventurer*. But what damped Sir Harry's spirits greatly was this, that his dear friend, John Murray, who was captain on our consort, had been washed overboard in the storm, and was no more ; and that the men might not see his grief, he went into his own cabin and shut the door, and I think there was no sad heart on board but his.

Presently Rodrigues came to my side, and, says he—

" Now is the time to win the hearts of these men. I shall get leave from the captain for them to go ashore ; do you give them something to make merry with."

I agreed to this with all my heart, and fetching the bag of gold from my cabin which Sir Bartlemy had sent, I bade him distribute every farthing amongst them ; and this he did, giving every man equal share, so that each got over a pound, for there was the value of two hundred pounds in the bag, and the companies numbered eight score, as near as may be.

When he had thus made the " dividend," as he called it, Rodrigues told them that it was

I who gave the money out of love for them,
and the hardships they had borne on my
account. Whereupon Ned Parsons cried he
would do as much again and a hundred times
more for so generous a gentleman, and bade
his comrades give me a cheer, which they did
with all their lungs, and three times. And I
thought this Ned Parsons was a good friend
to me, but he was not.

CHAPTER V.

SIR HARRY gave leave that all should go on
shore who had a mind to, save only such as
Parsons and Rodrigues should need to keep
on board the *Adventurer* and the *Sure Hawk* for
their protection; and Rodrigues bade all be
gone, saying that he and Ned Parsons would
watch the two ships during the night. So
the men went off in the barge, one batch after
the other, and last of all Sir Harry himself
went also to refresh his spirits after the grief
of losing his dear friend; and Parsons rowed
him to shore. There were then left on the
Sure Hawk none save Rodrigues and I. And
I being heavy with sleep (it being by that
time nine o'clock, as I think) threw myself on
my cot within my cabin, and fell off in a doze.

While I lay there Rodrigues came to my cabin and saw me by the light of the lamp, as I found out afterwards.

But presently awaking, I rose up and went out on the deck, feeling the want of fresh air. And indeed the night would have tempted most men to go forth, being very fair and the moon vastly bright, as it is in those parts.

There was not a soul on the deck, for Rodrigues, seeing me asleep and all clear, had gone into the captain's store-room to pilfer a bottle of wine; and so without design I sauntered on till coming, as chance would have it, to the main-mast of the ship, I came to a stand, and leaning my back against the mast so that I faced the moon, I fell to meditating on my lot. Whilst I stood there I heard the dip of oars; then the chink of glass as Rodrigues set down his bottles right over against where I stood, but on the other side of the great mast, and after that he went to the side and called over, "Come up, Ned.

I've that will make us merry, though we be
not ashore."

"For all that I would rather be ashore with
our mates," replies Parsons in a grumbling
voice as he comes up the side.

"And so we will, man, and many a jolly
night will we spend with our mates—when
we have no secrets to keep," replies Rodrigues.
"Here we have it all to ourselves, and need
fear nothing if the drink do give a loose to
our tongues."

"Where's Pengilly? He went not ashore,"
says Parsons, when he had tumbled over the
bulwarks on to the deck.

"Asleep in the coach where you see the
light burning, and is sound as a log. Sit you
down here, and we shall see him if he comes
out, which is not likely."

So they sat down together on a chest
facing the roundhouse, and just on the other
side of the mast where Rodrigues had set the
bottles, and presently began to drink and talk ;
yet still I kept where I was, with my back

against the mast; firstly, because the moon
seemed to spread a calm over my mind which
I cared not to dispel, and after that because I
became curious to know what they had to talk
about

" Well," says Parsons, in a more cheerful
tone, after taking a drink, "how goes it?"

" Famously," replies Rodrigues, clacking
his tongue against his teeth and pouring out
more wine.

" Have you sounded the men? Have you
opened out to them of our project?"

" Nay; not yet. Nor have you, I hope,
or they will blab everything before they get
sober again. I bade you keep a still tongue,
Ned."

" And so I have. There's been other
matters to think on. A rare time it has been
with us to keep the ship afloat. But I did
my part of the business."

" And bravely, I warrant. Tell me how
you did it, Ned."

" I caught him a stroke on the head with

a crow as he was at prayer, and heaved his body out into the sea by the galley port." 'Twas thus he had cruelly murdered Captain Murray.

" No one saw you ? "

" Never a soul. He was missed in the morning, and all think he was washed over by a sea."

" Well, there's one out of the way. 'Twill be Smidmore's turn next."

" When ? " asks Parsons.

" That's as hereafter may be. I'm for leaving everything till we have provisioned at Trinidado."

" And I'm for going at it at once. Curse this hanging fire when there's prize to be taken, I say. Now Murray is out of the way you will be made captain of the *Adventurer*, and I reckon I shall be master in your place on the *Sure Hawk*. We are well armed and ammunitioned, and shall not lack provisions. Then why should we wait till we've been to Trinidado, I want to know ? "

"Because we should have to victual again before going round to the South Sea, and we want no one to get wind of our intent before we're ready to fly our colours. It would be folly to spoil the venture for the sake of a week or two. Besides, we know not how the men will take it."

"How do we stand for men?" asks Parsons, in his grumbling tone again.

"Why, there's Black, and Jarvis, and Kelly, and all those of our old crew who served with us before—they may be depended on."

"That's thirteen men, and we two make fifteen, all told."

"These men, though they pretend to believe that we are going up the Orinoco after a mare's nest, are not such fools as to think that I design to end my days there."

"Ay!" says Parsons with a laugh, setting down his cup again. "Nor would they have been fools enough to engage on any such silly venture unless they felt sure something

F

better was to come of it. Well, there's fifteen
—go on."

" Of the rest there's two score as desperate
fellows as ever trod a deck, and ripe for any
mischief."

"Would to Heaven we could have raked
up more like them."

" The rest are fools; but sturdy, good seamen, for all that."

Here I was reminded of what I had previously remarked—viz., that there were two
sorts of men in our crew and no third. One
set were reckless, dare-devil, cursing rascals,
and the other were as simple-minded as any
children ; but, as Rodrigues said, every one a
hale, good seaman. And this was due to the
cunning of Rodrigues, who, by reason of his
knowing the parts to which we were bound, had
been entrusted to choose a crew likely for the
purpose.

" Well," says Parsons, " here are five-and-
fifty men to back us at a sign, and a match for
all the rest with their captain and your Pengilly

as well. Now, here's my plan, Rodrigues, and if you will hear me you shall own that it is better than all your fiddle-faddle of waiting for this, that, and t'other."

" Well, out with it, Ned. You know that I have never refused to listen to advice, nor to act on it when I saw it was good; else had we never won our way."

" That's true, and I own but for your cursed cool judgment we should all have been strung up like so many weazles."

Over this interchange of civilities they drank another cup and shook hands. Then Parsons started off in high good humour :—

" Here's how I see it. Sir Harry will make you captain of the *Adventurer;* for why? There's no man so fit; and he'll very like make me master of this ship under him, as being best able to navigate her and the like. The men will be fairly divided between the two ships as heretofore. Now, as soon as we set sail I shall make it so cursedly uncomfortable for the foolish fellows of my crew that they shall pray to be

F 2

exchanged into your ship. To this I shall per-
suade Sir Harry, taking in their place all those
men disposed to our design."

"So we get all the simpletons under me,
and all the desperadoes under you," says
Rodrigues.

"That's it. And matters being so, I will
open out our scheme to my crew, who will jump
at it like sharks. Then the first calm night
will we order things so that my men shall board
your ship after binding Sir Harry, and make
prisoner every mother's son : which done, you
shall ask the company plump out whether they
choose to join in our venture and make their
fortunes, or whether they stick to their articles,
and will go a searching for gold where there's
naught but serpents and fevers. Who will
refuse to join us then, eh ? "

"Sir Harry, for a surety."

"Then overboard he goes, and away we
sail south with joyous hearts, and no more
dallying."

Rodrigues took the time of drinking another

cup to consider. But little as I knew of this strange matter, I felt sure he would not agree to this proposal (being a very subtle, painful man), for if he thus parted with all the men proper to his desperate enterprise, what was to prevent Parsons deserting him and going whithersoever he pleased with his desperadoes?

"Yes," says Rodrigues, " your scheme might succeed, but it will be better to turn the tables about so that you send all the dependable men to me, and I send the others to you."

Parsons made no reply to this, whereby he revealed the secret treachery that was in his mind. But Rodrigues taking no notice of this, though he must have perceived it, continues cheerfully, " No, Ned ; on second thoughts that plan will not do. For taking the men unprepared in this way, a score of them may hold on to the hope of getting treasure in Guiana, and so rally round the captain. Then may we have to throw them overboard as well as the captain, which will be a great loss to us. For we can make no great success with small means, and it

will never do to start short-handed. Besides
this," says he, " the men pressed into our
service by the fear of death will never serve
us as willing hands would."

" Why, that is true," says Parsons, who
clearly did not relish the idea of his own
scheme being acted upon contrariwise. " You
always had a better head for these matters
than any of us. So let us hear how you would
act."

" In this wise," says Rodrigues. " As soon
as we set sail from here—you on the one ship
and I on t'other—we will secretly show the
dullards the folly of seeking wealth in Guiana,
when they can enrich themselves tenfold without leaving the ship, or encountering any of the
hazards and hardships of going a-foot through
those fearful wilds. And first will I win over
Pengilly, who is ripe for this enterprise. When
I am sure of him, Sir Harry shall be got rid of,
and then will Pengilly take his place as commander, being nephew to Sir Bartlemy, whose
ships these are. So without the loss of one

man shall we have gained our way, and all willingly will obey his directions."

"So far so good," says Parsons; "but how is this to advance us? Are we to take for our share no more than what he chooses to give us as his officers?"

To this question Rodrigues made no reply. And this silence perplexing me, I cast my eye sidelong to see if they had moved away. And then I perceived what it was had stopped his tongue.

The moon had shifted during their conversation (of which a great deal for the sake of brevity I have not set down), and whereas at the beginning it had shone full on my face, it now struck me somewhat on my left side. So that there down on the deck I spied my shadow revealed beside the great mast, and Rodrigues had spied it also. For before I could turn my head, I felt his long, bony fingers upon my throat, and then the flash of his dagger in the moonlight caught my eye.

CHAPTER VI.

Now, I had not stirred a hair's breadth the whole time this Rodrigues and Ned Parsons were discussing their affairs; and thus was I standing, with my back against the great mast and my feet a couple of spans away from it, when Rodrigues takes me by the throat, flashing his steel before my eyes, as I have said, and, at the same moment, Parsons, slipping his foot betwixt my legs and the mast, fetches me a trip which brings me plump down on my back. Then, in a twinkling he throws himself upon me, and had certainly done my business with his jack-knife (both having lugged out upon catching sight of my shadow), but that Rodrigues, catching his arm back, cries—

"Hold, Ned! Don't you see that this is none but our friend Benet Pengilly?"

"I see well enough who it is," answers Parsons; "but he is a spy for all that, and shall pay for stealing on us. Let go my arm, Rodrigues!"

But this Rodrigues would not, being just as quick to foresee results as Parsons was to lose sight of them.

"Don't be a fool, Ned!" says he. "How could he have stolen on us, and we sitting with our eyes on the cabin? He was here from the first, and I do not blame him for picking up what we were careless enough to let fall. And what harm in that? He has but learnt what we intended to tell him. Would you ruin everything by spilling his blood, when his loss would draw suspicion on our heads, and set all our mates against us with mistrust? Had it been another he should have died, and I would not have left the business to you neither; but the moment I got my hand on his throat I saw it was our friend."

"That may be," says Parsons; "but, curse

me! (adds he) he shall give me some better assurance that he intends to stand by us in this matter ere I let him rise."

"Nay," says I, "you shall get nothing from me by force;" and, getting my hands under him, I flung him off like an old cloak, and sprang to my feet. "Now," says I, "what is it you want of me?"

All this passed as quick as the words will run, so that the whole business was not more than a minute or so in the doing.

"Well done, Pengilly!" cries Rodrigues. "I like you the better for this taste of your manhood. I never mistrusted a brave man yet, and here's a proof of it now," and with that he sticks his dagger in the deck, and seats himself on the chest, with empty hands, bidding Parsons, as he was a true man and not a born fool, to do the like, which he presently did, sticking his jack-knife in the deck, and sitting alongside of Rodrigues; and, to show I feared neither, I seated myself betwixt them.

"Now, Ben," says Rodrigues, clapping me on

the knee, cheerfully; "what's it to be? You have heard our design. Do you stay in the Canaries, or go with us to the South Sea?"

"What to do?" I asks; for this question did still perplex me.

"What to do? Why, to get gold, to be sure."

"I thought you had decided not to set foot ashore," says I.

"And so we have; for what Englishman has ever got gold that went out of his ship to get it? The fools have thrown more gold into Guiana than ever they have taken out of it, a hundredfold."

"Ay! And gold is not the only thing they have thrown away," says Parsons, "but many a good and honest Englishman's life as well."

"For every man that has come home," says Rodrigues, "a hundred have been left behind— slain by Indians, stung by serpents, dead of fevers, or slaves to the Spaniard."

"And them as do come home are none the better for having gone thither," chimes in t'other rascal, " as we do testify; for here am I short of one eye, and Rodrigues a sight to see."

"That there is gold in Guiana no one can doubt," says Rodrigues; " but the only men who can get it are the Indians, and their only masters are the Spaniards and Portugals."

"Then where did you get the treasure you brought to England?" I asked.

" Why, from the Spaniard, to be sure, and as fairly as he got it from the Indian."

"Ay! and fairer," says Parsons; "for we got it by straightforward and honest fighting."

" And if we were more lively in our attack," puts in Rodrigues, " 'twas because their galleons were unwieldy with their weight of gold."

" I count we do 'em a service to ease them of their load," says Parsons, "for they have more than they can carry with comfort " (this with a laugh at his own joke).

"Ay! but our love doesn't end there; for, look you, Ben, which is the better—to let your uncle's ships and treasure be cast away in the Orinoco, to lead eight score men to misery and death in those fearsome wilds, or to carry them back home, every man rich for life? To suffer the Spaniard to carry that gold into Spain for the encouragement of Papistry and devilish cruelty, and the furnishing out another Armada, or to take it away from them for the benefit of our country and the honour and glory of our king?"

And in this manner they carried on the argument a long while, one playing the part of marrowbone to the other's cleaver, while I sat in silence and lost in wonder, like one who should of a sudden see a strange new sun rise up in the sky. At length I found the sense to speak, and, says I—

"But how can we attack the Spaniard when we are at peace with Spain?"

"Why," says Rodrigues, "peace there may be in these waters, for that matter; but there is no peace below the line, as every one does know."

"Nay," says I, "'tis nothing but piracy you offer."

"You may call it what you like," says he, "but I think it no shame for any man to walk in the shoes of Drake and Candish."

"'Tis a hanging matter, for all that," says I, still objecting.

"A hanging matter for those who fail to take home gold, but a knighting matter for those who do, as witness Sir Francis and others less nice than he. But 'tis the same all the world over, whether a man undertake to find gold or to cure bunions. Raleigh gets his head cut off for failing, and Master Winter is made a knight. And quite right it be so, for it puts a check on men from hazarding foolishly, and encourages them to push their fortunes with zeal, when the chance is on their side."

"And this is the long and short of it," says Parsons, bluntly, for argument was not to his taste. "Are you with us, or are you not?"

"I am with you," says I, and upon that we joined hands—all three.

And in thus readily falling in with this villainous proposal I was moved, not so much by Rodrigues, or his subtle arguments, as by my own fierce and lawless spirit, and a certain brutal craving and lust of blood and treasure, which, Lord forgive us, urges too many of us to cruel pursuits, no whit more justifiable in the eye of God than piracy.

CHAPTER VII.

WE stayed at Fuerteventura nine days, and then
made sail, being again in good condition and
nothing lacking, and shaped our course for the
West Indies. And as Parsons had foreseen,
Rodrigues was appointed captain of the *Adventurer*, while Parsons took the place of master
on board the *Sure Hawk*. This pleased the
Adventurer's company vastly, for all looked upon
Rodrigues with open admiration, backed up by
secret hope; and, indeed, there was no man
more proper for this post.

No sooner had we quitted our anchorage than
we began, Parsons and I, to work upon the
minds of those foolish fellows who had to be
prepared for that change we intended to bring
about. So now Parsons, instead of painting the

glories and delights of Guiana, as he had done
with a very free hand, when inducing them to
leave their fishing villages and join our ships,
now treated all such glories with derision, telling
them they were like all to get a good deal more
than they expected, and thrusting his tongue in
his cheek with a wink of his one eye at me for
all to see. Whereupon these fellows did begin
to scratch their heads and think they had been
hoodwinked, and led into a business which had
been better left alone. And from that he went
on to tell of all the horrible beasts and worms
there existed in the marshes of those parts; the
poisonous fruits in the forests, all so like the
wholesome that one never knew whether his meal
was to give him strength or burst him open by
its venomous swelling; of the cannibals, whose
shoulders grew higher than their heads, and
whose arms were two fathoms long; and such-
like wild stories. If any one doubted the truth
of what he said, he would appeal to one of those
men who had previously voyaged with Rodrigues, and these, seeing which way the cat

G

jumped, confirmed him in every lie, no matter
how outrageous. Then he came gradually to
talk of Hawkins and Morgan, and fellows of that
kidney, exalting them to the skies—in fine, we
carried this business so well that by the time
we arrived at Trinidado there was not one man
aboard the *Sure Hawk* but that heartily wished to
rove the South Sea for gold rather than to seek
it in Guiana; yet, for all that, a good half of the
crew were staunch and faithful to our captain,
and prepared to die with him in the wilds; nor
would they listen to anything in his disfavour,
or any project of desertion. And the reason of
this was that Sir Harry Smidmore, being of a
lively and sanguine temperament, and having
unbounded faith in the success of his enterprise,
had ever a cheerful and kind word for his men,
and neglected not to comfort the company in
every possible way, so that he won all the hearts to
him that had any decent feeling. Indeed, as the
fresh sea air purged away my splenetic humour,
and the society of sturdy men inspired me with
a wholesome shame of those contemptible

humours which were bred by solitude, I no longer harboured an envious jealousy towards Sir Harry, perceiving plainly how far above mine were his claims to the love of Lady Biddy Fane. Feeling thus with regard to him, I could neither wish to do him a mischief myself, nor to see him come to harm by other hands. Yet every day it became more obvious that a cruel end awaited him. There was no chance of his forsaking the expedition into Guiana to become a pirate on the high seas, and it was therefore clear that he must be privately got rid of to avoid a mutiny amongst simple good men who were staunch to him.

I own I was greatly perplexed over this matter, and more than once I was on the point of revealing the conspiracy to him; for I felt that, if he were murdered, I should, in a manner, have his blood upon my conscience; but as many times was I deterred from this confession by recalling my oath to Rodrigues, and by a certain sense of honour which may exist even amongst such rogues as we were. And so I was terribly

G 2

put to it all the time we lay at Punto de Gallo, revictualling and making the final preparations for going up the Orinoco.

We lay off Punto de Gallo eight days, and the men of both ships mingling, Ned Parsons and Rodrigues found occasion to lay their heads together pretty frequently; and this boded me no good, for Parsons had ever kept a jealous and suspicious watch upon my movements, and must have perceived my growing love for our captain. On the evening of the eighth day, we three being ashore together, and come to a spot free from observation, Rodrigues says—

" If this breeze holds, we are likely to sail to-morrow; and as we may not get another chance of conversing privily, let us settle what's to be done, and how we are to do it when we are aboard."

" Ay, we've had enough shill-I-shall-I," says Parsons, in his surly tone.

" We should have been further off from success if we had gone a shorter way to work, Ned," says Rodrigues, " as you know well enough, though you won't own to it. If we had followed your advice and thrown the captain overboard when we left the Canaries, half the men would have been against us, and looked upon the first storm that came as a judgment on us. 'Tis no good setting men to a task before they're prepared for it. Now there's not a man aboard the *Adventurer* who is not thirsting to get at the Spaniard."

"You've had them all to yourself; but it's another matter aboard the *Sure Hawk*," says Parsons; "there's two score of half-hearted fellows amongst us that were better at home."

"That's as you think, Ned. What say you, Pengilly?"

"The men's hearts are as stout as ours," says I; "and as ready to meet the Spaniard as any of your crew. I'll answer for them."

"Perhaps you'll answer for their flinging the captain overboard when the time comes?" says Parsons, with a sneer.

"I'll answer for you, Parsons, if there's a cowardly murder to be done; but for no one

else on board the *Sure Hawk,*" says I. " I
warn you, Rodrigues, that if you attempt the
life of Sir Harry, you'll have two score of us
to settle, with him and Benet Pengilly among
the number."

" There, didn't I tell you as much ? " says
Parsons, nudging Rodrigues.

Rodrigues frowned on him to be still, and,
turning to me, says, calmly enough—

" What do you mean by that, Pengilly? "

" I mean this : our captain shall not be
murdered," says I.

" And how can you prevent it, pray ? "
asks Parsons.

" There'll be plenty of time to warn him
before you can silence me, Parsons."

" Didn't he swear secrecy by the cross,
Rodrigues ? "

" Yes, I did," says I ; " but I'll break my
oath rather than have murder on my conscience ! "

" Conscience ! How long have you been
troubled with that commodity ? " asks he.

"Fool! you be still," cries Rodrigues, stamping his foot. "Haven't you sense enough to see that Pengilly's warning saves us from the very thing that I have dreaded all through? I know the mischief of having discontented men in a crew."

"Settle it how you will," says Parsons, with an oath, getting up and turning his back on us. "Curse this dodging backwards and forwards, say I!"

"If the captain were out of the way, and you took his place, as lawful representative of your uncle, the men would do your bidding, wouldn't they, Benet?" says Rodrigues, in a friendly tone.

"No doubt," says I; "but I will not have any hand in this business if violence is to be done to Sir Harry."

"Then what do you propose we should do?" asks he.

"He lies ashore to-night: why shouldn't we sail without him?"

"That's better than ever!" cries Parsons,

turning round. "Leave him here to send a king's ship after us. A plaguey good notion, that," and he burst out into a horse laugh.

"That won't do, Ben," says Rodrigues; "as Ned says, we should have a man-of-war sent after us, and so have to fight English as well as Spaniards. I think I can offer something better than that;" and, drawing me aside that Parsons might not hear, he dropped his voice and said, "Supposing, when we are out at sea, we tell the captain of our determination to go roving, and ask him to join us?"

"He will refuse : that's certain."

"Very well; then let us give him one of the ships and let him go with as many of the men as choose to join him. What say you to that?"

I agreed to this readily; for it seemed a better way out of the mess than any I had imagined.

"Good," says he; "so shall it be. Now, leave me alone with Parsons. He is a self-willed, headstrong fellow; but I know how to manage him, and I promise you I will make him hear reason."

So I left them, never dreaming but that Rodrigues, for his own interest, was dealing fairly in this business, and speaking his mind honestly.

That night our captain brought aboard an Indian Cazique named Putijma for our pilot. This man told us that the true mouth of the Oronoque and the best for us to enter was in the Boca de Nairos, and about thirty leagues south of Punto de Gallo; and thither it was agreed, the breeze remaining prosperous, we should sail the next day.

When this news was imparted to our company there was a great cheer, and every man set to with a will getting the ship ready that she might sail at daybreak; and the sky being very fair and clear they worked all night to this end, and there was such tumult of men coming on board, shouting of orders, and getting things in their places, that no sleep was to be got.

A little before daybreak I turned out of my
cot, and, going on deck, found that some were
already aloft shaking out the sails, while others
were heaving up the anchor, and all singing
of sea songs, and as merry as any grigs. Ere
yet the sun had risen our sails filled; we left
our anchorage, and, looking out, I spied the
Adventurer, her sails spread, following pretty
close in our wake. Then, the light growing
amain, I perceived one strange face amongst
our company, and then another, and after that
a third and a fourth, and so on, till I numbered
a full dozen; yet these men were not so strange
to me but that I recognised them as being
part of the crew of the *Adventurer*. Upon
this, suspecting mischief, I cast my eye about
for those men whom I have spoken of as being
staunch and loyal to our captain, and not one
of these could I find. In this I saw clearly
the villainy of that subtle Rodrigues, who, by
thus shifting the crew, ensured his plan against
opposition, for not one man now on board the
Sure Hawk could be counted on to side with

the captain in going into Guiana, whereas all
would readily agree to ridding themselves of
him in order that they might follow their own
lawless bent uninterrupted; meanwhile, by his
own persuasion and the influence of the rascally
crew on the *Adventurer*, those simple fellows
from the *Sure Hawk* who still held to an honest
course could be easily won over to his purpose.
To make sure that the change on board was
not due to accident, I sought out Ned Parsons;
but the rascal, seeing me coming, feigned to
be mightily busy, so that I could not get a
word out of him any way, which served to
convince me of his treachery. Getting no
satisfaction from him, I went into my cabin,
and there, sitting on my cot, I turned the
matter over in my mind, and, after looking at
it this way and that, I resolved I would go
and warn Sir Harry of his danger; for, as I
had told Rodrigues, I was prepared to break
any number of oaths rather than be a party to
a foul murder. And, lest I should be credited
with more generosity in coming to this decision

than I deserve, I will here confess that I was
not unmindful of my own peril. For, if it
served the purpose of these desperadoes to throw
our captain overboard, why should they spare
me? I laid no faith whatever in the promises
of Rodrigues; nay, I was inclined to believe
Ned Parsons the honester rogue of the two.
I knew that all he considered was how to
advance his own fortune. Had the crew been
more difficult to seduce and less disposed to
become pirates, then it would have served his
turn to carry out his original project, and give
the enterprise a fair face by appointing me, as
nephew of Sir Bartlemy Pengilly, their generalissimo; but now that it was clear the whole
body of men needed no such countenance to
their project, it would be expedient to get rid
of me as well as Sir Harry. So to the captain,
who still lay in his cabin, I went, and asked
him if he knew of the change that had been
made.

"Ay, Pengilly," says he, cheerfully; "I
ordered it so. Parsons tells me that there is a

lawless spirit spreading amongst the men on the *Adventurer*, and he picked out certain of them as being the worst. These Rodrigues begged me to take with us in the *Sure Hawk* in exchange for those he thought might bring the rest to a healthier way of thinking on the *Adventurer*."

"That villain, Rodrigues!" I exclaimed. "I saw his devilish hand in this. We are lost!"

"Lost! What do you mean by that?" asks Sir Harry, bating his breath.

"I mean that you have parted with the only honest men in the crew, and have none but ruffians left about you."

"Nay, you wrong them. Desperate they are, for who but desperate men would dare a desperate enterprise? But they are honest— I'll answer for 'em. They have sworn to follow me, and they will."

"You will be lucky to get away without such followers," says I; "but, in truth, I doubt if we do ever set foot again on dry land."

Sir Harry could not speak awhile for astonishment. At length he says, speaking low—

"Are you sure of this you tell me, Pengilly? Are you honest with me?"

"I'll say nothing for my honesty," says I; "but I'll swear to the truth of what I tell you. There's not a man but is already a pirate at heart; and they only want a signal from Rodrigues to kill us and hoist the bloody flag."

Sir Harry started up, and took a pace or two across the cabin; then, coming to a stand, he turns and says—

"No, Pengilly; I can't believe this. Tell me you have tried to fool me, and I'll forgive you."

"Nay, but you must believe me," says I, "or you cannot escape else;" and then I laid bare all that I knew, with my own share in the villainous scheme, not sparing myself the shame of this confession. He listened to me patiently, but when I came to an end he says, with passion—

"God forgive you, Pengilly; for my ruin is on your head."

But presently, growing calmer, for I made
no attempt to defend myself from this charge,
he adds—

"Take no heed of what I said, Benet. You
have done no more nor less than I, or a better
man than I, could have done in your place.
You risk your life in trying to save mine,
whereas you might have made your fortune
(though I doubt if you could ever have enjoyed
it) by betraying me."

He held out his hand, and I took it. Then,
in a more cheerful and vigorous tone, he says—

"Come, we are both in the same pickle; let
us see how, perchance, we may get out of it."

Then we set our wits to work that we might
discover how we two were to overcome the craft
and force of all those hardy villains that were
against us. I was for knocking Parsons on the
head, taking the navigation in our own hands,
and running the ship ashore, or on the first
shoal we came to; and I think Sir Harry
would have acted on this design, but that it
pleased Providence to give us no chance that way.

CHAPTER VIII.

OF a truth none are so suspicious as those who should be suspected, and losing sight of this fact was our undoing.

To begin with, 'twas a silly thing to go into the captain's cabin at that time; it was still more imprudent to sit there with him discussing our means of escape. For it happened that Ned Parsons, seeing me no longer inquisitive about the shifting of the crews, became curious to know what had become of me, and presently sighted me sitting, as I say, with Sir Harry. Doubtless Rodrigues, in his place, would have taken some crafty means of discovering our design and circumventing it; but this Parsons was of another kidney, and prone to reflect upon the advisability of his actions after they were performed rather than before. Wherefore, at the first sniff of danger, he goes below, collects a dozen choice rogues, and these having gone into the armoury and furnished themselves with weapons, slipped on deck, and in a twinkling rushed into the roundhouse and fell upon us. We were the less prepared for this attack because the fellows, having no shoes to their feet, came on noiselessly along the deck; and indeed, from the moment we first spied them to the time they were in the coach, there was barely time for Sir Harry to whip up a short sword for his defence, and I a spyglass that lay on the table. Sir Harry ran the first of the party through the vitals, and I managed to lay Ned Parsons' head open with the perspective; but we could do no more, for we were thrown down by sheer force of weight and numbers, and after that our bootless struggles did but prolong by a few minutes the work of binding us hand and foot. From these bonds there was no escaping ; Ned Parsons himself, with the blood yet trickling down his face and

H

grizzled beard, making fast each knot and test-
ing its security. When this was done, he went
out on the main deck and spoke to the men
crowded there, and they replied with a great
cheer, and so betook themselves to their work,
shouting and talking among themselves with
much content. But to make more sure of us,
and that all might see we were not contriving
our escape, this Ned Parsons hauled us out of
the roundhouse into the midst of the deck, and
there we lay in the burning sun all that day,
and none had the humanity to give us meat or
drink, though they for the most part made
themselves as drunk as beggars by midday.
Nay, when Sir Harry, who had been as kind to
these wretches as any man could be, asked one
to give him a cup of water, the villain would
not, but replied, with a brutal laugh, that he
should have more water than he could drink at
sundown, by which cruel speech we perceived
that our fate was sealed, and that they only
awaited the occasion of Rodrigues' coming on
board to cast us into the sea.

The breeze continuing very fresh, we pressed onward; but towards evening the wind abated, as it does in these latitudes about sundown, the sails flapped against the mast, and the anchor was dropped.

Soon after this Rodrigues came aboard, and first he consulted with Parsons, who had contrived to keep more sober than the rest; then they held a council with all the men in the fore-part of the ship, after which Rodrigues comes to us, with his hat in his hand, as civil as may be, and with a wicked smile on his face that showed all his pointed teeth, so that with his hypocritical air he did look more like a fiend than a man.

"Gentlemen," says he, "I am sorry to tell you we must part. The men, one and all, have resolved to seek their fortunes elsewhere than in Guiana, and lest their design should be distasteful to you and lead to any further breaking of heads or spitting with steel, they would have me, as being now chief in command, drop you overboard with a shot tied round your

necks. I have done my best to alter their dis-
position, but the most they will consent to in
your favour is that you shall be allowed to go
your way in consideration of your giving them
free permission to go theirs, with a solemn
promise on your part that you will hereafter
do nothing, if you have the chance, to bring us
to the gallows."

"Do with us what you will," answers Sir
Harry.

"Ay, and be cursed for the villain you are,"
adds I.

"As you do not refuse the offer it is my
duty to make, I shall hold it you accept," says
Rodrigues, taking no notice of me; " betwixt
gentlemen no formalities are needed. It is understood that in accepting your life you agree
to the conditions, and this understanding will
be as binding on you to do us no harm—if, as
I say, you get the chance—as though you had
put hand and seal to a bond."

Then making us a bow, he went back to the
men, who, on hearing what he had to say, gave

another cheer, and some set about lowering Sir
Harry's own barge, while others went below and
fetched up all manner of stores to put in it. All
being in readiness, we were taken to the side of the
ship, bound as we were, and with a rope reeved
through a block at the yardarm, we were hauled
up and lowered like cattle into the barge that lay
alongside. Then for the first time we perceived
that the land was distant no more than half a
mile or so. After us the Indian Cazique Putijma,
whom, as I have said, Sir Harry had brought
aboard at Punto de Gallo for a pilot, was made
to come down in the barge, and so half a dozen
seamen in that boat that had brought Rodrigues
from the *Adventurer* towed us with a line to the
shore, the crew giving us a jeer as we sheered
off, and Rodrigues (with a bow) wishing we
might have a pleasant journey to Manoa, and
find a kind reception and store of gold there.

Having brought us to land and made our
barge fast, the boat's crew, with somewhat more
humanity than their fellows, bade us good-bye
and god-speed, and then pulled off quickly

back towards their ship, for there was no moon
that night, and it was now grown so dark that
we could but just descry the two ships lying off
in the bay.

All this time Putijma, who was unbound,
had sat in the barge with his knees up to his
chin in profound silence; for such is the stoic
character of these Indians when overcome by
misfortune from which they see no escape. But
now Sir Harry, who spoke Spanish, addressed
him in that tongue, begging him to cut our
cords, and this he did; but it was yet some
minutes ere either of us could move, so benumbed
and stiff were we with our long confinement.
When I got the use of my limbs and hands,
I drew a drachm of liquor from the puncheon
among our stores, and gave it to Sir Harry, who
was thereby much refreshed. Then did we get
out of the boat to exercise our legs, and finding
the sand still warm and pleasant with the sun's
heat, we lay ourselves down to sleep, there being
no better thing to do. But first I got from
the boat a couple of muskets, with powder and

ball, and two hatchets, that we might not be unprovided against the attack of wild beasts or cannibals in the night if any such there might come upon us.

But Putijma never stirred out of the boat, nor could Sir Harry any way cheer him out of his despondent mood; and the last I saw of him he was still sitting with his knees huddled up to his chin, and so we presently fell asleep.

We slept soundly, and nothing disturbed our slumber all through that night. The sun was some degrees above the horizon when I awoke, and a smart breeze ruffling the sea. Sitting up I looked out for the ships, but they were no longer in the bay; yet methought I spied one sail on the horizon to the south. Then I got upon my feet and looked for the barge and the Indian Cazique, but trace or sign of either could I see none. I rubbed by eyes and looked again; then I ran a hundred yards along the shore eastwards, and again as far to the west; for I could not at once realise that this man was treacherous to us. But 'twas all in vain; he was nowhere to be seen.   So I roused up Sir Harry, telling him how the Indian had played us false and gone away with the boat, which was our only means of getting back to Trinidado, and like distracted creatures we ran along the shore a mile one way and a mile the other, hallooing aloud, as trying to cheat ourselves with the hope that Putijma had slipped away by accident, and drifted into some creek.   But at length we gave up the quest, and stood gazing before us as still and silent as statues of stone, quite overwhelmed by this last stroke of misfortune.

And thus were we two poor men abandoned on an unknown coast.   I say we two poor men, for now were we levelled to the same degree by a cruel fate, being possessed of no more than a gun and a hatchet apiece besides the clothes we stood in, and with the same dismal expectation of perishing unfriended in a wilderness.

CHAPTER IX.

WE FIND OURSELVES ON A DESERT ISLAND, AND LITTLE COMFORT BESIDES.

AFTER a while we returned to the place where we lay during the night; and, looking about us, found that the cruel Cazique had taken away the keg of powder, the puncheon of rum, ay, the very bread we had brought for our refreshment on landing; thus robbing us of our present subsistence and the means of procuring other.

Seeing this, Sir Harry threw himself on the sand and sobbed out aloud; for as yet he had suffered never any hardship or disappointment. But it was otherwise with me, for many a time had I endured privation and known no hope. Yet did it move my heart to see a strong man, and one naturally light of heart, gay, and of high spirit, so abased; so I sat down beside him, and, laying my hand on his shoulder, spoke such comforting words as my tongue, unused to such exercise, could command. And this may seem strange, seeing that hitherto I had borne him no love, but rather jealousy and hatred. But you shall notice that misfortune doth engender kindness in hearts the least susceptible, so that a man who would jostle another and show no manner of kindness and civility, both being strong, would yet bend down and gently succour him who fell across his path from weakness; for our sympathy is with those weaker than ourselves, and not with those of equal hardiness; and this, I take it, is the reason of the great love of strong men for weak women, and the wondrous tenderness of women for those cast down by sickness.

Sir Harry would not be comforted; but shaking my hand from his shoulder he cries—

"Ay, 'tis easy to make light of another's burden!"

"Nay," says I, "am I better off than you?"

"Ay," says he, "for you have but changed one form of misery for another. These woods

for you are as good as those you left in Cornwall; your prospects here as good as they were
there.   But I! what have I not lost by this
change?   All my fortune was embarked in those
ships; and with them I lose every hope—fame
and riches—my sweetheart.   All! all!   What
now have I?"

"The hope of getting away from this place;
the hope that—that she may wait faithfully
your return."

"And what if, by a miracle, I get from here:
can I hope to recover my fortune?   I must go
a beggar back to England; nay, a debtor for
the ships of Sir Bartlemy that I have lost.
And think you if my sweetheart in pity would
make me her husband, I would be her pen-
sioner, dependent on her bounty for the bread I
eat?"

To me this seemed an overstraining of sentiment; for I would have been content to take
that dear girl for my wife, rich or poor; nay, I
could not believe that any sense of dependence
or bounty could exist in the union of two who

love entirely. But I would not contrary him
by speaking of this, which he would but have set
down to want of decent pride and self-respect on
my side.

"There is no hope—no hope!" he continues, bitterly. "I am undone by my enemies,
and you are one of them—a man I have sought
only to help—a base wretch who would not
speak a word to save me from my undoing."

I held my peace, as I had before when he
spoke after this sort. For partly I felt that I
deserved reproach, and partly I saw that he was
beside himself with despair. So I let him be,
that he might vent freely all his passion. But
he said no more; and for some while he lay
there like one who cared not to move again.
Then getting upon his feet savagely, as though
ashamed of his weakness, he says—

"Let us go from this cursed spot." Then,
looking about him in bewilderment, "Where
shall we go?"

Be a man never so wretched, he must eat
and drink; so I told him we must first of all

seek a stream to quench our thirst ; and the
land to the west looking most promising, I
settled to explore in that direction ; Sir Harry
being indifferent so that we got away from this
unlucky place where we had been set ashore.
We took up our axes and muskets—which the
thieving Cazique had left to us because they lay
under our hands, as I may say, and he feared to
awake us—and marched onwards, keeping to
the sand, which was very level and firm, the
tide being at low ebb. We kept on this way
for best part of a league, and then the shore
becoming soft with a kind of black mud, we
were forced to seek higher ground ; and here
our progress was made very painful and slow by
reason of the scrubby growth, which was mighty
thick and prickly, so that we were torn at every
step. To add to our discomfort, the sun, being
now high, shone with prodigious heat upon us,
and parched us with thirst. There were woods
at hand, but here the thorny brush was so high
and closely interwoven that we had to use our
hatchets to make any way at all, and then were

we no better off, but worse ; wherefore we were obliged to return to that part where the earth was less encumbered. Some of these brambles had thorns two inches long, and curved like great claws ; and one of these tearing my leg gave me much torment. As the sun rose higher, so our suffering increased, until, after marching best part of two hours, we were ready to drop with fatigue. Fruit there was in abundance, spread out temptingly under our feet ; for nearly every bush bore some sort of apples or grapes ; yet dared we not eat any for fear of its being venomous. Of this venomous fruit I had heard the seamen who had travelled in these parts tell, and how a man eating of it will presently go raving mad ; and I pointed out to Sir Harry, who would fain have slaked his thirst with this growth, that we had as yet seen neither bird nor beast, which argued that this food was not wholesome.

However, about midday, when we were as near spent as any living creatures could be, we came to a turn in the coast where the character of the growth changed; and here we found a great herb with leaves spreading out on all sides; but every leaf was a good twenty feet long and half a fathom across, so that it gave us ample shade to lie in; and never was man more content than I to get out of the sunshine. To our still greater comfort, Sir Harry presently spied at no great distance a low-growing thicket, in the midst of which grew a fruit that he knew for a pine-nut, which is a fruit bigger than any that grows in England, of a yellow complexion, and scaly without, but of an excellent condition within. Cutting it in half with his knife, he gave me one part, and bade me eat it without fear; and this I did, though not without compunction, but I found it truly as he said, both meat and drink, and the most delicious ever man did eat, with no ill effects after.

We rested ourselves some while, and then being much refreshed continued our journey over very fair ground, but yet keeping very nigh the water; and so rounding a headland, and facing pretty nearly due west, we perceived another

headland across the water, but at a great distance, which led us to conceive that we were
upon one of the mouths of the Oronoque, which,
as we know, disembogues itself by many issues
into the sea over a length of an hundred leagues
and more along the coast of Guiana.   And that
this was a river, and not an inlet of the sea, we
proved by tasting of the water, which was still
running out very troubled ; it was not salt and
bitter, but yet too thick and brackish to drink.
And now the trees approached the water-side,
some hanging over, with thick growth every-
where ; and though I know English trees well,
and the different sorts of herbs, yet all here
were new to me, and I saw none that I could
name.   For prodigious height and girth I never
saw the like of the trees, which were besides
wondrous fair to the eye, but painful to get
through by reason of their great abundance,
and the maze of vines and bramble (as I must
call them, knowing not their names) which netted
them together.   Surely to one come there for
pleasure and to satisfy his curiosity, there was

on all sides something to please and interest, there being no end to the variety of flowers and fruits, their colours and forms; but to us, who were mainly concerned to discover where we were situated, we did wish best part of these. trees and shrubs further.

We made our way onwards for two hours more, yet the land on the other side of the river appeared no nearer, for the rivers in these parts have no parallel for volume; and then we came (God be praised) to a small stream running from the interior, which we found at some little distance inward to be very sweet and good, so that we drank of it our fill. But what pleased me as much as the discovery of this water was the print of a cloven foot in a slough, hard by, which I judged, by the form and size, to be the foot of a swine; and so it proved, for going still further, but with caution, along the edge of this marshy land, we perceived a whole drove of this cattle stretched out in the warm mire, grunting from time to time as pleasantly as any English hogs. Seeing them thus within range, Sir Harry, ere I

I

could check him, cocked his piece and let fly;
and though he killed one dead on the spot, yet
was I sorry he had spent his fire on this quarry,
for I believe I might have knocked one on the
head and done for him with a blow of my
hatchet; and now were we left with only one
charge of powder and ball to meet any emer-
gency.

We dragged this beast, which was a boar pig
of some ten score, as I reckoned, away from the
morass, which I dreaded to stay in for fear of serpents or other noxious beasts; and finding a place
near the river high and dry, we resolved to stay
there the night, for the day was nearly spent, as
were we likewise.   Here Sir Harry set about to
get some dry fuel and make a fire, the while I
skinned our pig, and a marvellous thick hide he
had; and so much the better was I pleased, for
I saw that with this hide cut in thongs I could
make us a good gin to entrap other swine when
we had occasion for them, also a sling for killing
birds, and other things necessary to us in our
forlorn, destitute condition.   Sir Harry got some

dry rotten wood, and grinding a little to powder
he set it in the pan of his firelock, and snapping
the cock twice or thrice succeeded in setting it
burning : then blowing the ember gently.on other
rotten wood, and that on dry leaves and such-
like, he in the end got a flame to put to his bon-
fire, and over this on pointed sticks we held
some slices cut from our swine's ham ; enough
not only for our supper, but to serve us cold on
the morrow ; and well it was we did so then, for
the next morning the carcase I had hung on a
tree overnight was all green, and so foul we were
fain to cast it in the river to be washed away
with the current; but that which we had cooked
was sweet and good, though mighty tough eat-.
ing.

But I must tell of the strange way in which
we were awakened that morning, which was by
the crowing of a cock, and surely nothing, in
this land so full of unlooked-for things, could
be more unexpected than this familiar, homely
cry. We two started up together at the sound,
rubbing our eyes to be sure we were in a strange

country and not at home in England. But
again this bird crowed, and casting our eyes
about, there we spied a fine red cock perched in
the boughs of a tree with three pullets on one
side of him and two on the other, all as com-
fortable as you please, and not yet astir, for the
day was scarce broke. Upon this we concluded
that there must be human habitation near, and
overjoyed at the hope of seeing fellow-creatures
in a land where we had thought to be all alone,
we started to our feet and hallooed with all our
might, not reckoning that the fellow-creatures
might be cruel Indians who might murder us,
and mayhap eat us afterwards for our pains.

However, though we hallooed till we were
hoarse and could whoop no longer, answer came
there none, except a clucking of the fowls, who
seemed to be at a loss what we were crowing
so loud about. Yet from the presence of these
fowls and the swine—which seemed to us not
natural inhabitants of these parts, we clung
to the idea that some sort of fellow-creatures
were near, and so with a more cheerful heart

than I, for one, had yet felt since we were put
ashore, we continued our march when we had
eaten and drunk to our satisfaction.   But first
we took of the thongs I had cut from the
swine's hide and stretched to dry between two
stakes, one apiece to serve as belts in which
to sling our hatchets, another which I had
fashioned for a sling, and two or three besides
to serve for what occasion might arise.   The
rest we left behind us, marking well the
spot.   Our ham steaks we covered up in cool
leaves to keep them fresh, and hung them also
to the thongs about our middle.

That night we came to a point projecting
into the midst of a vast expanse of water, and
seeming to cut the river into two, for we found
that there were, as I may say, two currents—
one running to the south-east, and the other
north-east—so that we concluded we were not
on the mainland at all, but upon an island in
one of the great mouths of the Orinoco.   This
was made evident as we proceeded, for still
marching with the water on our left hand, our

faces were turned to the east and not to the
west, as at first; and, in short, on the third
day of our march we came again to the ocean,
and about midday on the fourth to the very
spot from which we had started.

In all this time we had seen no human
creature, nor had we met—thank God!—with
any serious accident, though inconveniences not
a few; and not the least of these was a mul-
titude of flies and stinging gnats, especially upwards away from the sea, which were a great
plague to us, and especially to Sir Harry, who
had the more tender skin, and was tormented
to that degree that he could get no peace night
or day for the intolerable itching and smarting
of their punctures. Nor did we meet any great
beast, save a huge water-lizard that is called
a cocodrill, which lies in the waters of these
rivers and looks like nothing on earth but a
log of timber at a distance. Birds there were
in plenty, and with my sling I brought
down enough for use, and more; and to speak
of all the fruits here were a waste of time.

Suffice it to say that we lacked nothing to satisfy our appetite, and came to no harm by what we ate of strange things, for we were careful to eat of no fruit or herb but such as we found the swine and other animals feasted upon.

CHAPTER X.

AND now, being come back to our starting-place, we had to consider our position and what we were next to be at. I say we, but in truth I might say I had to consider these things, for Sir Harry seemed to have neither care for the present nor hope for the future, and do what I might to bring him to a more cheerful complexion, it was all to no purpose.

"What is there to do in this cursed island," says he, "but to eat and drink and sleep till we die?"

"The more reason," says I, "for devising some means of getting away from this isle to where we may do better."

He stretched out his hands towards the sea that lay void before us, and laughed bitterly.

"Nay," says I, not to seem discouraged, though, indeed, my hopes were but slight; "it is not so impossible as you think. Take it that the day we left Trinidado the gale was in our favour, we could but have made twenty or thirty leagues at the outermost. Now, say that the river to the north is three leagues broad, we may yet, by taking the current at our highest point, contrive to make our way across on some kind of raft, using a bough for paddle. There is nothing lacking to make us a raft."

"Well," says he, "say by good hap you cross the river and get on another isle—what then?"

"Then," says I, "will we make our way to the north of that island, and cross to a third, or a fourth, after the same fashion, and so get on till we come to that part of Guiana due west of Trinidado, whence may we with no more difficulty cross the strait."

"Suppose, after all," says he, "that we get to Trinidado—what then? Shall we be better off there than we are here? We run a fair chance of being captured for slaves by the Portugals, to be sure."

"Also," says I, "we run a fair chance of escaping them and being picked up by some English ship putting in as ours did to revictual."

"Allowing that your fondest hopes be realised," says he, "is our case mended? Is it worse to sleep away our lives here than to be taken into England as a raree show for men to laugh at and women to pity? No," says he, with more passion than he had yet shown; "no, I say! It is not better, but a hundred times worse, and I for one will never go back to be scorned for a silly fellow who could not hold his own."

It was not for me to reproach him, for had I not also abandoned myself under adversity? I was convinced, and so I am now, that despair is a malady of the mind as much as is ague a distemper of the body; and though men say one should not give way to despair, but should overcome it by an effort of will, yet I say that if the will be attacked by a great shock and

enfeebled by misfortune, it is powerless to exercise its function. For such as suffer from this
disease of the mind there is no help from within,
but its only succour is from without. Wherefore, the kindly ministrations of a friend will do
as much to restore health in this case as the
help of a doctor in any other. For this reason
I bore patiently with Sir Harry in his morose
and sullen humours, and sought all I could to
divert his spirit from brooding over misfortunes
not to be undone. But I think all that I did
in this way produced me more good than it did
him; for whereas he continued despondent and
dull, I grew more cheerful and humane. I
waited upon him like a servant, and this service,
with my pity to see a young, fine man so cast
down, engendered a feeling of love in my breast
such as I had never before felt for any man.
Nay, I even looked to getting with him back to
England, and seeing him married to Lady Biddy
Fane, without any feeling of jealousy, being not
only more gentle of heart, but more reasonable
of mind than heretofore, thank God!

At this time we stayed on high ground to the south of our territory, over against that part where we first found the pine-nut; not only because of the shade we got there from the sun, but by reason that it was adjacent to the stream of good water, and not far from the fen where the swine came to wallow, and where there was abundance of fowl and fruit good to eat.

While we were here, Sir Harry fell sick of a fever, bred partly, as I think, from his low, desponding spirit, and partly from the vapours that rose from the marshy valley below. When I found he could no longer sit upright and began to wander in his speech, I took him on my back, and, by stages of a dozen yards, carried him away from that unwholesome spot right down to the sea-shore, and there, finding an easy slope, I laid him down, and, as speedily as I could, set about making a kind of house to shield him from the sun. The night being fairly light, by dint of many journeys to and fro, and much toil, I planted a dozen stakes in

the sand, bending them down till they joined at
the top, in the form of a great **A**, and binding
them to a cross tree, then I thatched this frame-
work with those long and broad palmetto leaves
of which I have spoken. Here he lay as com-
fortable as might be for one in his burning
condition, the sea breeze passing through the
shelter and tempering the heat of the sun.

He could eat nothing; however, I made shift
to stew a fowl in the shell of a gourd, and
when the broth was cold I got him to drink
it, for he had a perpetual thirst; and that his
drink might be cool and refreshing, I went a
score of times during the day almost to the
source of the stream, where the water was of
the best. Of such fruits as were good also I
gave him, particularly the apples from a low,
square-boughed tree with egg-shaped leaves,
which is called, I believe, guava.

And now I prayed to God that this man's
life might be spared, and that I might not be
left alone, which more than all proves the great
and good change which had been wrought in

my heart since the time when I sought but to escape from the society of mankind, and wished harm to all men, and this one above all.

At the end of seven days' very painful watching, Sir Harry's disorder took a turn, and soon after he began to mend (thanks be to God!) so that he could take meat instead of slops to his diet. Yet was he greatly changed, his skin having lost its freshness and healthful colour, and his face much wasted. Also he was very weak, and for days lay exhausted and unable to move, yet with his eyes wide open and very bright. After a while I persuaded him to rise in the cool of the morning and evening, and then would he take a turn, leaning on my arm. And though he said nothing, I perceived he recognised the love I bore for him, and was grateful for my care. What pleased me vastly was to observe that a change had been wrought in his spirit; it seemed as though his sluggish indifference had been purged away. When the fever had quite left him, his eyes continued bright and quick, and there was in his face an eager expression, telling of an anxiety which only exists where there is hope. But what his hope was he told me not. This encouraged me to believe that he designed leaving the island (where there was, as I could see, naught to hope for), and not dying there, as he had at first resigned himself to. I again began to meditate on the means of reaching Trinidado, but I refrained from opening the subject yet awhile, because he was still too feeble to undertake the fatigue of it.

One day, when I had returned to the hut by the shore from the inner parts, where I had been planting a snare to catch a pig, I found Sir Harry absent; but soon after I heard him shouting, and, turning my eyes, I spied him running towards me along the sand with something in his hand, which, as he came nearer, I perceived was the stave of a barrel.

" Look at that," says he, with much emotion ; " there have been men on this island before us. Up in the wood there is a broken barrel; this is a stave of it. Men brought it here."

"Why, for a certainty," says I, "this wood never sprang out of the earth fashioned thus!"

"No," says he, "nor did the pigs on this island spring out of the earth."

"What do you mean by that?" I asked, perplexed by this observation.

"I mean," says he, "that the men who came here to fetch water in that barrel left the swine and the fowls to multiply against the time they should come here to revictual. I thought as much as I lay there in my sickness hearing the cock crow, and now I have the proof. Do you doubt it, man—do you doubt it?"

"Not a whit," says I; "and I wonder I have not drawn the conclusion before, for I remember now how Rodrigues told me it was the habit of pirates, who fight shy of towns, to provide for themselves in this wise."

"Then you think," says he, eagerly, "that they are pirates who came hither?"

"Ah, and not honest men; that is my fear," says I.

"And I trust they be pirates, and not honest men, if they are to come here again," says he; "for then may I get back all I have lost, and more to boot."

"As how?" says I, not without trouble in my mind.

"By the same means my fortune was taken from me—by strategy and force."

"Surely you would not become a pirate—you, a gentleman of birth and breeding?"

"And what was Drake but a gentleman?" says he; "and Candish: what of him?"

I shook my head, and heaved a sigh to hear this argument from the lips of my friend, which I had listened to from such a rascal as Rodrigues.

"Why," says he, in a rallying tone, "you were not so squeamish aboard the *Sure Hawk*."

"No," says I; "but I thank the Lord I have not taken His warning in vain."

He laughed scornfully, as though thinking my peril had made me prayerful, and caressing the barrel stave with his hand, lifted his head

J

and scanned the sea, as already expecting the return of those pirates we talked of.

"And is your fortune all you expect to get by becoming a pirate?" I asked, laying my hand on his arm.

"What more do I want, forsooth?" asks he, lightly.

"Why, sir," says I, "the peace of mind to enjoy it."

"As for that," says he, "however I get it I warrant it shall bring me more enjoyment than I can expect stopping here, or going back to England a beggar."

"Are you so daunted by the outset that you despair of getting gold honestly in Guiana?"

"Hum!" says he; "I cannot see that it is much more honest to take gold from the Ingas of Manoa, who have never done us harm, than from the Spaniard, who has sought to undo us with his flotilla; but, be that as it may, you will show me how we are to get to Manoa, who are not yet beyond the mouth of the Oronoque, ere I give that enterprise the preference."

"Single-handed we can do nothing, but I will answer for it that my uncle, Sir Bartlemy, instead of being discouraged by our first failure, will be more inclined to persevere in it. You know his nature as well as I do. A reverse does but strengthen his determination, as a bite infuriates a bulldog."

"That is true," says he; "he is an Englishman to the very marrow of his bones."

"Well, then," says I, "shall he not fit you out another expedition?"

"Why, man, how can he? Nearly all he had was united to my fortune in buying the two ships I have lost, and in equipping them. He is a ruined man. Ruined by me!"

"If he lacks money, other shall be found. He will move heaven and earth to save you from the disgrace of sinking to the level of such wretches as Morgan and Sawkins, and this Rodrigues."

In this sort I reasoned with him persistently,

J 2

till at length, seeing that I was not to be shaken off by argument, he turns about and says—

"Look you, Pengilly, I will never go begging in England, even for a second chance to be cast away on this island. I cannot easily consent that another should beg for me; for a craven I must appear in either case. But since your mind is set on this thing, go you to England without me; and if any, for my sake, will make this venture, lead them hither; then, if I be still here and alive, I will attempt this expedition to Manoa. Nay," he adds, interrupting me, when I began to protest that I would not quit him; "leave me here and go about this business as you will, you shall still be the more generous of the two; for I swear to you that if the worst pirate that sails the seas comes here I will cast in my lot with him, whether you accompany me or whether you refuse to take part with us."

Seeing him very stubborn and resolved upon this point, I then began to think seriously of getting away as best I could; for, thinks I, 'twere more humane to leave him here alone, with the chance of bringing him succour and the means of honestly escaping from his solitude, than to rest here inactive until perchance there comes some villainous sea-rover with whom he shall take his departure. For my own part, I had now no leaning to piracy; for, though I loved the Spaniard no more than any other true Englishman may, yet I knew full well that Rodrigues and such fellows would not question closely whether their prey was Spanish, but would pillage and sink any craft that sailed so that it had not the strength to resist attack.

So, going along the border of that upper stream, which in my ignorance I will call North River, I came upon a great tree that was dead and decayed about the roots, so that it needed but little cutting to make it fall, and that close to the water. This tree was fully three fathoms in girth, and proportionately tall, straight, and fair, decayed only where the humours of the earth had attacked its base, light and very proper in all ways to my use. Wherefore I set to work, and, cutting on that side I wished it to fall, I felled it with no very great difficulty. When it was down I found the upper part sound, as I expected, and not so hard but that with patient labour I succeeded in cutting two lengths, each of five fathoms long. These two lengths I set side by side, the thicker end of one against the thinner end of the other; then I got me a quantity of those long vines which the Indians call lianas, which are very stringy, and tough as good hemp rope, and with this I bound my timbers together in a hundred places, but separately, so that if by chance one broke the rest would still hold. But I must tell you that for the greater convenience of working these huge logs I launched them separately into a shallow before I began to bind them about, which was well, for I could never have moved them else. After that I sought out two slight trees of hard growth that were not more than thirty feet high, and, cutting them down, I trimmed them into two poles, each

four fathoms long. Then, midway in the length
of my logs, I made two holes—one in each,
and parallel one with the other. To do this I
jagged the mouth of my musket barrel about,
grinding each jag into a sharp tooth with a hard
stone, by which contrivance I made a tool to
serve in place of an auger. When I had pierced
the logs right through I enlarged the holes by
making my musket barrel red hot in a fire, and
working it about in the holes. Into these
sockets I fitted my two poles, using every device
I could think of to make them firm and secure;
and this being done, and both poles standing
bolt upright, I turned the logs on their side so
as to get the ends of the poles within reach, and
these ends I bent until they met, and so bound
them together with lianas to make them bite still
closer in their sockets, and also to be a support
one to the other against the gale, for they were
to serve me as a mast. For, by the time my logs
were cut, launched, and bound together, as I
have shown, I had come to the conclusion that
it would be better to venture the whole voyage

by water, keeping as near as might be to the main, and taking advantage of favourable breezes, rather than to abandon my raft on the other side of the river and make my way onward by land to that point nearest Trinidado, as I had first meditated on, for I knew not what other great rivers there might be to cross, nor how many rafts I might have to make ere I got to my journey's end; and the difficulty of making such a raft, rude as it was, no one can conceive but those who have had a like difficulty to contend with. It cost me four months and ten days of painful labour to achieve that which I have set down.

During this time Sir Harry had not been idle; and though he could not honestly encourage me with a hope of bringing my business to a happy issue, yet he helped me with a willing heart, and said nothing which might discourage me neither. But he was as firmly fixed in his intent as I on mine, and rarely worked up the river with me, lest in his absence the ship he expected might come and go away again.

Anything he could do within sight of the sea he did, and this was no trifle. Here every day he provided food for our necessity, and in his spare time he fashioned me a long yard for my mast, and, which was more, he made a shoulder-of-mutton sail—to rig on my mast like a lateen on a zebec—of long reeds very ingeniously woven together. Also he devised two vessels to contain fresh water for my use by stripping a couple of hogs from the neck downwards without cutting the skin. These skins he turned inside out, scraped off all the fat carefully, and then steeping them in the sea until they were well cured, and afterwards washing them some days in the stream of fresh water, they were found good and sound, each holding a good hogshead of water.

Besides this, he cut a vast quantity of pork steaks and cured them in the sun, which may be done without corrupting the flesh if it be laid where the sun is hot and the air dry. Moreover, he saved all the bladders of hogs that he killed, blew them out, and coated them over with a

sort of pitch to preserve them from the attacks
of flies and insects.   This pitch comes from the
sea of those parts, and is washed ashore by the
tide, and being melted before a fire, it is as good
a pitch as any in the world.   These bladders I
tied on to the extremities of long poles lashed
crosswise to my raft to serve as a sort of buoys
to bear up that side to which the sail inclined,
and prevent the raft from capsizing in a sudden
squall.

I bound some bundles of reeds transversely
to the logs to serve me as a deck, and many
other provisions I made, such as a great stone at
the end of a line for an anchor, a paddle to serve
as a rudder, etc.   In fine—not to weary the
reader with tedious descriptions — just ten
months to a day from the time we were set
ashore all was made ready for my departure.

And now, taking Sir Harry's hands in mine
and pressing them close, I begged him to come
with me.

"Look you," says I, "this offer is not un-
premeditated on my part.   All through I have

borne it in mind, and for that reason have I
measured my boat and all things to serve two
rather than one. Here is provision for both and
to spare ; the breeze is favourable, and all things
promise a prosperous outcome. Do, then, be
persuaded by me, dear friend, to share my
fate ; if not for your sake and mine, then
for those who love you in England and are
eagerly hoping for your return."

He was not unmoved by this address, and
the tears sprang in his eyes as he wrung my
hand in silence ; but he shook his head the
while.

" No," says he, presently ; " no, Pengilly ;
you know not the pride of my heart. It would
kill me with shame to show myself a beggar
there," turning his eyes towards the north. " I
am a ruined man—ay, ruined body and soul—
for I feel that I am unworthy of your love.
Go ! "

" Nay," says I, " let me stay, that my persuasion may work on you. I left my offer till
the last, hoping——"

"I know," says he, interrupting me. "You hoped that the prospect of being left alone, coming to be reviewed suddenly, would shake my resolution. But I have foreseen this. I saw that you were preparing for two to make voyage on the raft. I knew that you were not dwelling cheerfully day by day on the prospect of escape but to excite a desire in me to escape with you. I know what is in your heart, and have just sensibility enough left in mine to value it. But I will not go. I am resolved, and naught can shake my resolution from its centre. Go; and may God bless you."

So with a very sad heart I was fain to accept his decision; and shoving out into the stream I went down swiftly with the current, and had not the courage to look back on that poor lonely man I was leaving behind.

CHAPTER XI.

By making vigorous employment of my paddle, first on one side and then on the other, I continued to keep well in the midst of the river, and the tide then ebbing fast, I was quickly swept across the shallows at the mouth, and so out to sea.

And now I thought it proper to hoist my sail; so, laying aside my paddle, I drew up the lateen between my two masts till it was taut, and then making fast the liana found it acted well enough, for at once it filled out very full and fair to the breeze, which was blowing pretty brisk from the south-east.

But now my difficulties and troubles began, for I had no experience in the governing of a

sailing boat, and ere I had got to work at my
paddle, my raft veered round before the gale, the
sail flapping to and fro between the masts, and
I had all the pain in the world to get her head
round and my sail full again.   And when this
was achieved, I found a fresh fault, and this was
that my buoys were nothing near sufficient to
resist the pressure of the sail, so that they dipped
deep into the water, the poles to which they
were fastened bending to such a degree that I
expected nothing less every moment but that
they would snap under the strain, and the raft
capsize utterly, to my final undoing.   Wherefore
I was fain to abandon my paddle, and reef the
lower part of the sail to lessen the pressure, in
which time I again lost the wind ; so back to my
paddle and more labour to bring me round once
more before the breeze, etc.

By this time I perceived that the current of
the sea and my bungling together had swept me
far from the coast, and rather to the south than
to the north.   And to my great perplexity I
found that I could not get the wind in my sail

without drifting still further from the shore to the west; for if I steered to the north, then would the wind go out of my sail, and the craft, losing way, would drift with the current to the south, so that if I did nothing matters could be no worse. At last I was constrained to lower my sail altogether and seek to make head against the current by vigorous use of my paddle, first on one side and then on the other, as I say. And, lord! no man could be more encompassed with troubles than I was, or sweat more to overcome them than I did at this time. At length, from sheer exhaustion, I was fain to give over, and let my raft, without sail or oar, go whither it might. I sat me down on my deck of rushes, and casting my eyes towards the land was dismayed to find it but an indistinct line on the horizon (I having been out to sea now four hours or more), and to the best of my belief I stood further from Trinidado, after all my trouble, than ere I started forth. And let this be a warning to all men that they put not to sea ere they have learned to sail.

When I had refreshed myself with some water and one of my dried pork steaks (which, that they might not be perished by the sea water, I had hanged conveniently high on one of my masts), I rose up, and with a kind of desperate fury essayed again to make a proper course. First, I went at my sail once more, and when I found that of no avail, but rather the contrary, I seized my paddle, and worked at it like any galley slave; and though I could see no improvement, yet did I persevere diligently. Then, fancying the breeze was a little abated and blew from another quarter, I went (with a prayer) and once more lifted my sail, but that would not do; and so (with a curse) I dropped it and back to my paddle. In fine, to cut a long story short, 1 wasted my pains all that day, and had the mortification, as I sat down once more to rest my aching limbs, to find the land no longer in sight; nor anything else but the water all around me.

Seeing it was useless to work when I could no longer see for want of light (though not

more useless than before, may be), I lay me
down on my reeds (the sea, God be praised!
having subsided when the wind dropped to an
agreeable calm), and presently fell asleep.

The next day there was no need to experi-
ment with my sail, for not a breath of air
stirred; so I worked steadily at my paddle
pretty nearly the whole day, but I was forced
to desist in the noon for some time because of
the great heat of the sun, and that while I
sheltered myself under the sail, which was, God
knows, all the use it ever served me. All that
day I heard not a sound but such as I made
with my paddles, and the sea was like so much
glass extended about me, and a mist all around
the horizon caused by the sun sucking up with
his great heat the vapours from the water.
When the sun set, this mist settled over the
whole sea, so that I could see never a star to
cheer me, and this made me very sad and
prayerful, for it seemed as if a death-pall were
being spread over my unhappy being. Then
would I gladly have been back with Sir Harry

K

on the island; and thinking of him and our miserable estate, both alone, and like to perish without ever again hearing the sound of a cheerful voice, the tears began to flow from my eyes as from a woman's; and I do think I fell asleep weeping.

About midnight (as I reckon) I was awakened by the freshening of the breeze; yet nothing could I see. I groped my way along very carefully to my masts, that I might have them to hold by, for already the sea was rising; and it was well that I did so, for in an amazingly short space of time the breeze quickened to a gale, and beat the waters so high that I was like to have been swept away by the waves as they burst. I will not dwell on the increasing terrors of that night, for no words can describe the fury of that hurricano, or my dread lest the binding of my logs should be rent asunder and my frail resting-place part under me. And here let me observe that, no matter how a man may desire death at other times, yet in the hour of peril will he ever cling desperately to life.

When morning broke, my case was no better than in the night; and looking around me at the billows that threatened every moment to engulf me, I was appalled, and could but say, over and over again, "God be merciful to me!" For a long while I experienced neither hunger nor thirst; but only great fear and terror; but when nature began to crave within me, and I looked to see if I could get at my water-vessels, I perceived that they had been washed away in the night, for I had taken no precaution to lash them to the raft for safety. And also I noticed that my deck of rushes was clean gone and my outriggers broken. My only comfort was that the bonds of my raft still, for the most part, held good, though the straining of the timbers had loosened them, and it was clear they could support the rubbing of the logs and the wrenching of them but a little longer. I saw that if one or two at the end went, then all must go; therefore, as I crouched between the masts, I watched these bonds as a man may watch the preparing of a gallows from which he

к 2

is in the end to be swung off into eternity.
And after my raft had been shot down into a
great hollow, and thence rising up, met the
fearful buffet of another huge wave, I saw that
the end liana was burst asunder. "God be
merciful to me!" says I again, and with the
greater earnestness that I felt I might the next
moment be in His presence.

At this moment, above the tumult and rush
of the waves and wind, I heard a report like
the firing of a small piece of ordnance, and,
casting my eye in that direction, I saw, to my
vast amazement, a great ship bearing down
upon me, and not two fathoms off. And that
noise I heard was made by the splitting of her
topmast and its striking the side of the vessel
as it fell. Scarce had I seen this when the ship,
riding down on the wave, ground its foreside
against the end of my raft, and the next instant I found myself entangled in the wreck of
the broken mast with its yard, which still hung
to the ship by its cordage. Some of this cordage passing right athwart me, I sprang up and

clasped it; then, though as how I cannot tell, but as I best might, I climbed like any monkey upwards, getting no more than a dozen or so good thumps against the ship's side, and knocking the skin off my knuckles by the way, until I shoved my head above the bulwarks, where already two stout seamen were severing the broken mast from the cordage with hatchets. When these two saw me rise as it were out of the grave over the bulwarks, I say, they were stricken with greater terror than the fury of the tempest had inspired, and fell back from their business with gaping mouths and starting eyes; but as I tumbled over the side and threw myself on the deck, and they perceived I was no ghost, but only a poor shipwrecked wretch, they picked me up and bore me, into the roundhouse to their captain, for I had no power even to stand, being quite spent with my exertion and trouble of mind.

The captain spoke to me, but I could not understand him; for, as I afterwards found, he was from Holland and spoke Dutch, and I spoke

to him with no better effect, for he knew no
word of English.   Nor did any man on that
ship speak anything but Dutch, or understand
our tongue.   I tried to make him comprehend
by signs that I had ventured to sea on two
logs, but he could make nothing of me till we
got to Schiedam (which we did, thanks be to
God, in a little over eight weeks), where was
a man who spoke English.

The captain was very humane and kind to
me, and for my serving him on the voyage,
which I did to the best of my ability and cheerfully, he paid me at the same rate he paid his
other seamen, besides giving me a decent suit
of clothes, of which I stood much in need.
Through this good man's generosity was I
enabled to pay my passage in a galliot to Yar-
mouth in England, where, by the good help of
Providence, I arrived full safe and sound.

And there had I yet some pieces to spare
for my sustenance and to help me onward to
Falmouth.

CHAPTER XII.

I REACHED Fane Court eighteen months, as near as may be, from the time our first unhappy expedition set out.

When I asked for Sir Bartlemy, the hall servant seeing me all dusty with travel and out at heel, told me I must bide my time, as the knight and Lady Biddy Fane were at dinner.

"No matter for that," says I; "tell him his nephew, Benet Pengilly, is here, and I warrant you will fare better than if you kept him waiting for the news."

The fellow started in amaze hearing my name, which was better known to him than my face, and went without a word to carry the tidings of my return to Sir Bartlemy. Almost immediately afterwards my uncle came out into the hall, and as quickly after him Lady Biddy

—Sir Bartlemy as hale and hearty as ever, and Lady Biddy, to my eyes, more beautiful than before; but both pale and greatly amazed in countenance.

"Benet!" gasps the old knight, and that was all he could say. But he held out his hand, which I took and pressed with great love, for my feelings were much softened by hardship, and I was much grieved to think of the pain I was to give him instead of the joyful news he looked for. Lady Biddy stepped forward, and her face lighting up with hope, she looked for the moment as if she also might be kind to me, and welcome me for the sake of her lover. But of a sudden she checked herself, seeing my downcast complexion, and bating her breath, she says—

"Where is he? Where are the rest?"

Then says I, with as much courage as I could muster, but with pain that went to my heart—

"I am the only man who has come back." And with that I hung my head, not to see their grief.

" He is not dead—they are not all lost ! " I heard her say, in a tone that seemed mingled with a silent prayer to merciful God.

" No," says I; "Sir Harry is not dead. I left him out there in Guiana ; but for the rest, if they be lost, 'tis their just reward."

Then Lady Biddy burst into tears to know that her lover lived, and Sir Bartlemy, taking her by the arm and me by mine, led us into the dining-hall without speaking.

By this time, Lady Biddy's emotion being passed, and her pride returning, she took her arm from her uncle's, as if she would not accept of kindness that was equally bestowed on such as I.

"Sit ye down there, Benet," says my uncle, pushing me to a seat; "and now tell us all as briefly as you may ; for I perceive that the case is bad (with a plague to it!) though Harry live (God be thanked !); and if there be a tooth to come out, the quicker it's done the better."

Then I told the bare truth : how Rodrigues and Ned Parsons had led the crews astray and

set us ashore, and the means of my coming
again to England, in as few words as I could
shift with.   When I had made an end of this,
Lady Biddy was the first to speak.

"Why did not Sir Harry come back with
you?" says she.

"He scorns to come back a beggar," says I.
"He will never return to England until he can
repay his obligations to Sir Bartlemy and ask
you to be his wife."

This gave her great joy, admiring in him
that quality of pride which she cherished in herself, so that her eyes sparkled again, and her fair
bosom swelled with a sigh of satisfaction.
Presently she turned again upon me, her pretty
lips curved with disdain, and, says she—

"And you left him there in that desert
alone! Content to save your own life, you
abandoned him to hopeless solitude. Oh, that
I had been a man in your place!"

I hung my head again in silence, feeling it
were better to bear her reproach than to attempt
an excuse; for I could not trust my tongue to

reveal the main reason of my escaping, for fear I should betray his intention of turning pirate; and this, for the love I bore them, I was resolved to keep secret.

"Nay," says Sir Bartlemy, coming to my help, but with no great enthusiasm neither; "never beat the dog that comes home." He paused, and I could fancy his adding to himself, "Curse him, for a mean-spirited hound, all the same!" Then he continues, in a more hopeful tone, "If he had not come home, how could we have known of Harry's peril? Come, Benet; tell me that in coming hither you hoped to get succour for Harry."

"You might believe that," says I, "of a man with less heart than you credit me withal. I came to beg for help because Sir Harry was too proud to beg it himself."

"I knew as much," says he, taking my hand and shaking it heartily. Then turning to my Lady Biddy, "And now, my dear, what's to do? I have no money, and an expense I must be to you all the days that I live now that my all is lost, with a plague to those rascals that robbed me ! But you of your plenty will charter a ship to go out and fetch this poor man ? "

" More than that must be done," says I. " He will only accept such help as will enable him to recover all he has lost."

There was approval in Lady Biddy's looks when I said this.

" Odds my life ! he's in the right of it," cries Sir Bartlemy, bumping the table with his fist. " Plague take me if ever I'd come sneaking home with my tail 'twixt my legs like a whipped cur that has neither the stomach to bite nor to keep away from his sop. I mean nothing ill with regard to you, Benet," he adds, turning about to me, " for I hold you have done the part of a true friend and a good, and have shown more courage and high spirit in this matter than many another. Well, what's to do, girl, eh ? "—turning now to Lady Biddy, and rubbing his thighs with his broad hands cheerily.

Lady Biddy, with not less eagerness in her manner, looked to me, and nodded that I should speak all that was in my mind.

"As much must be found as has been lost," says I. "For nothing less in men or treasure will suffice Sir Harry to reach Manoa. And with that it is a venture, and naught can be done without God's good help, for never man saw a country so difficult to penetrate or such currents of rivers to mount. And first, money must be raised."

"Money shall not lack. I will venture my fortune to the last piece," says Lady Biddy.

"Ay, and so would I, if I had aught to lose," cried Sir Bartlemy. "But you, my girl, may well spare enough for this venture, and yet have as much to lay by for another, if that fail."

"No time must be lost," says I.

"Not a moment," cries Lady Biddy, starting up as if she had but to fetch money from her strong chest to accomplish all. "You must see about ships and men at once, uncle."

"Ay," says he, "but who is to command them, and carry help to your sweetheart in Guiana?"

Lady Biddy looked at him, and he at her, whetting his lips, as one with a dainty dish set before him that he would fain eat of.

"I'm an old fellow, but there's life in me yet: there's vigour—there's manhood," says he; "and if I decay 'twill be only for want of use. And I know the seas as well as any man, and I warrant me no crew of mine should take my ship from me, as from this poor lad, who put too great faith in the honesty of seamen. I dream o' nights of ocean seas; and feather beds I do hate more than any man can."

"Then why should not you command this expedition?" says Lady Biddy.

He tried to look astonished at this design; then putting his beard betwixt his fingers and thumb, and shaking his head doubtfully, he tried to look grave, but his merry eye twinkled with delight at this notion. Yet presently his chap fell, and he looked truly serious.

"My dear," says he, "what am I to do with you? I cannot leave a young girl alone in this place, and you have no relative but me, nor any steadfast friend to whom I may confide you, and a scurvy to it. Lord! I'd have done it, but for this plaguy obstacle."

Then Lady Biddy, as mad as he and as fond, cries—

"Do you think I will be left at home to mope, as I have in these past months? Nay— where my fortune goes, there go I also."

"And why not?" cries my uncle, banging the table again. "Was there e'er a better governor than Queen Bess, and she was a woman? And no queen that ever lived had a higher spirit or a braver heart than thou, my dear! Kiss me, for I love you. Now go fetch the chart from my closet. Benet" (turning to me), " you shall go with me and be my counsel (as much as you may, being but a poor sailor, I take it). We'll set to this at once; ships must be bought and men got—honest men—and none of your rascals who have come home with gold, and tell of getting it from the Ingas." In this way he ran on, till Lady Biddy came in, bringing the chart; and a very good chart it was, so that I had no difficulty in pointing out the island where we had been set ashore, as I have said.

Then did this uncle and niece lay out their plans gleefully as any children designing a holiday jaunt—reckoning nothing of the perils and terrors that I knew lay before us. But this sanguine temper was of that family's nature. And beautiful it was to see that graceful, lovely girl leaning over beside the old knight, following the course he laid down on the card—her face all aglow with eager hope and love, her eyes sparkling, and her rich, ruddy lips sweetly curved in a smile about her little white teeth.

I know not how it came about—whether it was the pang which shot through my heart as I reflected that this admirable creature was for another and not for me—that for his sake was she hazarding her fortune and life, while, if she thought of me, it was but with scorn; or whether my body was exhausted by the fatigue it had endured in hastening hither and my long fast (I had walked all night and eaten nothing but scraps of cow-salad torn from the banks), I cannot say; only this I know, that, while I sat there watching that sweet girl, a great sickness and faintness came upon me, so that I had to rise and go to the window for air.

Then Sir Bartlemy spying me, and how my face was white and the cold sweat standing in beads on my brow, perceived that I was sick. So he brought me a mug of ale and some meat, which were his remedy for all ills. But what did comfort more than these victuals was the kindness that filled Lady Biddy's heart when she saw my case. No angel could have been more tender. And while this mood was yet upon her, she said in my ear—

"Benet, I did you wrong in my too great haste; for I see now that you have served him with great love, and I must love you for so loving him."

L

CHAPTER XIII.

THE CROSSED HEART.

When two impetuous streams join and flow together, their course must needs be swift—whether to flow into the sweet and happy valley, or into the dark and horrid gulf. Thus while my uncle occupied himself in one matter, Lady Biddy busied herself in another, and both to the equipment of this new expedition; so that in an incredibly short space of time all provision was achieved, and we were ready to set out.

First there were ships to be procured, and seamen to serve them. For better choice, Sir Bartlemy journeyed over to Portsmouth, taking me with him, and a well-stuffed purse, together with a dozen lusty servants for our safe escort through those lawless and dangerous parts which lay betwixt Truro and Exeter, where no man rides safe.

Being come without mishap to Portsmouth,
Sir Bartlemy found an old acquaintance of
his, a broker and a very honest man, and with
him we went and examined all those ships that
were to sell, choosing in the end two that were
after his heart; excellent fair ships too, sound
and swift, that had sailed the seas, one two years
and the other four; for Sir Bartlemy would
have no new ships, but only such as had stood
the test of tempest, and were fully seasoned.

While this was a-doing I made a discovery
which gave me no little concern. The broker
would have us look at a French ship, albeit Sir
Bartlemy declared he would trust himself in no
timbers that had not grown in England; however, to humour him, we went to the side of the
harbour where she lay. But at the first sight
of her my uncle turned up his nose, and began
to find a hundred faults, finally declaring that
nothing good ever came out of France save her
wines, and that it would be time better spent to
drink a pint of Bordeaux than to go further
with the examination of such a cursed piece of

L 2

shipbuilding. With that he invited the broker
to crack a bottle in an adjacent tavern, which
they did without further ado. But something
in the look of this ship arousing my curiosity, I
feigned to have no liking for wine, and getting
the broker's leave to visit the ship, I hired a
wherry and was carried to her.

La Belle Espérance was her name, and she
was painted quite fresh in very lively colours,
after the sort of French ships ; but for all that
when I got on board my suspicions were stronger
than ever ; for the make of the ship (being little
altered) was, as I may say, familiar to me.
And straight I went into the coach, and so to
the little cabin on the larboard side, and there
on a certain timber I sought and found this
mark, cut deep in the wood :—

Then I knew beyond doubt that this ship,
despite its new name and fresh paint, was none

other than the *Sure Hawk*. For this crossed
heart was my cipher (making the letters B. P.
after a fashion if looked at sidelong) which I
had engraved with my own hand and of my
own invention.

I needed no further proof, but, being greatly
troubled, went straightway ashore. And there
finding occasion to speak privately with the
broker, I questioned him concerning this ship:
how long she had lain at Portsmouth, etc.

"Why, sir," says he, very civilly, "she has
been here three weeks, and no more. To tell
you the truth, she was a French pirate, though
I said nothing of that matter to Sir Bartlemy
to add to his prejudice. But she is a good
ship, and was taken by some honest English-
men trading in spices."

"And what was the name of their ship
who took this?" I asked.

"That cannot I tell you," he replies, "for
their ship was so disabled in the fight that they
had to abandon her and come home in this."

"Do you know these men or their captain?"

"No, sir, for they were of Hull; but I believe the captain's name was Adams, for I heard of him yesterday."

"In what respect?"

"It was in this wise. He bought a new ship of a brother broker here—the French vessel being not to his taste, nor big enough for his purpose—and sailed it hence to fit out and victual at Hull, where his crew would fain see their friends; and to Hull we thought he had gone. But my friend having necessity to go to St. Ives, in Cornwall, did there see this very ship, and Captain Adams with his men ashore, all as drunk as any fiddlers; which amazed him, so that he spoke of it as a thing not to be understood."

But I understood this well enough, and therefore I laid the whole matter before my uncle, and would have had him go with me to St. Ives, where I doubted not but we should find Captain Adams to be Rodrigues, and so lay him and his rascally crew by the heels, besides seizing his ship for our redress.

But my uncle would not agree to this.

"For," says he, "in the first place, it is a tedious business to stir the Admiralty to our profit, and in that time this Rodrigues—curse his bones!—may get wind of our intent and slip through our fingers; and, secondly, I hold it best not to stir up a sleeping dog, but to get on while one is safe. Added to which, every moment's delay is as much as a year of suffering to Harry."

To this I could make no objection, so I agreed to keep what I knew secret. But I perceived full well that my uncle, had he not openly expressed to his friend such contempt for the French ship (as he thought her) would have let Sir Harry wait until he had proved her to be the *Sure Hawk* and brought Rodrigues to justice, for he was very revengeful when roused, and full of hatred for the man who cheated him; but because he feared ridicule—having condemned that for worthless which but twelve months before he had bought for the best ship ever built—he would do nothing.

For which weakness, God knows, he was fully
punished in the end.

Our business being brought to an end at
Portsmouth, we sailed our new ships into
Falmouth Haven ; and their names were the *Sea
Lion* and the *Faithful Friend*. And here were
piles of merchandise waiting to be shipped, for
Lady Biddy Fane had faithfully bought and
prepared every sort of things in just proportion,
as before our going Sir Bartlemy had set down
in an inventory ; and none but a capable woman
of stout purpose and strong heart could have
done so much.

To work went all to get this store aboard—
the very house - servants being pressed into
service (such as they could compass), under
the direction of Lady Biddy ; yet could not all
be done in a day, nor much less than three
weeks, and no time lost.

All this time my mind was exceedingly
uneasy, lest Rodrigues should hear of our expedition, and seek to do us harm. And with this
dread I made inquiries (privately) if during my

absence any one had called to see me, and I found that no one had asked for me. This put me in a great taking, for now I felt sure that either Rodrigues or Parsons and his men were at Penzance. For otherwise to a certainty the wives and sweethearts of those men drawn from Penny-come-quick and Truro to our first venture, hearing as they must of my return, would have sought me for tidings of them. And if they were in communication with those men, then must our enemies know that I had come back, and that another expedition was fitting out. I knew the nature of Rodrigues — subtile and daring wretch!—merciless in the pursuit of plunder, and bloody as those beasts of prey which will kill, though they be too surfeited to eat, their quarry.

At length all was ready for our departure. Lady Biddy having paid off all her servants (save a good wench whom she took with her) sent her plate and treasures to a silversmith in Exeter ; and so, to cut this matter short, put her estate in the hands of a trusty steward, and bade farewell to her friends. We all got on board; my uncle and Lady Biddy in the *Faithful Friend*, which was the larger and better ship of the two, and I in the *Sea Lion*. For though Sir Bartlemy would have had me with him, and Lady Biddy said nothing to discourage me therefrom, yet did I feel that it would be better that I should not see her, fearing her beauty might stir up the passion in my breast, and lead me again into evil thoughts.

It was arranged that, the breeze proving prosperous, the next morning we should depart at break of day; and licence was given to the crew to make merry on board till ten o'clock, that they might start with a cheerful heart.

Now while the men were rejoicing after the fashion of mariners, there comes a wherry alongside with a woman in it; and this woman cries out to know if Jack Stone is aboard of that ship or the *Faithful Friend*. There was no man of our crew with that name; but this woman being comely and buxom, with a merry face, the men did pretend that Jack Stone was aboard, but too drunk to stir; and with that they asked her to come up and give him a kiss for farewell.

"Why," says she, coming up the side without more ado, "do you start so soon? Jack told me yesterday you did not set out for a week."

"We sail at daybreak, sweetheart," says the gunner, taking her about the waist.

. And this is what she had come to learn, as I feel convinced; for as soon as she had heard as much as was to be pumped out of these fuddled fellows, she left them, and was rowed ashore, never having again asked after the man she called Jack Stone.

The purser being a sober man, I asked him if he knew the woman, and he told me he knew her well for a Penzance woman.

"Then," thinks I, "Rodrigues has brought his ship round to be near us, and he has sent this woman for a spy. From Penzance she has come on this mission, and to Penzance she has returned; and so God help us."

CHAPTER XIV.

WE set sail at daybreak with a fair breeze, and if this had held on, then had we got safely on our way, escaping all danger from our enemy; but being only a land wind, such as frequently blows towards the sun at its rising, we found ourselves an hour after clearing Falmouth Haven in a little chopping gale, where we had much ado, by tacking this way and that, to make any progress at all, to our misfortune. While we were thus pottering to and fro, a sail appeared coming down the Channel, whereupon, my fears being that way disposed, I took it into my head at once that this was Rodrigues's ship from Penzance, there having been ample time during the night for the wench who had come aboard to take him intelligence of our intent to

sail. Then I begged Captain Wilkins, an excellent good man as ever lived, to let me have
the ship's barge that I might go speak with my
uncle; to which request he acceded instantly,
and the barge being lowered and manned I was
carried to the *Faithful Friend.* Here, taking my
uncle aside, I laid out all that had happened the
night before, and pointing to the sail bearing
down towards us, I gave him my apprehensions,
begging he would put back into Falmouth
Haven while we yet might. But this would he
not do.

"What!" says he, "put back because a
sail is in sight! Why, at that rate might we
never get out of Falmouth. Never yet did I
put back, for I count it the unluckiest thing a
seaman may do; and in this case 'twere nothing
short of folly and rank cowardice; for our foe,
if foe he be, is but one, and we be two. You
have done your duty, Benet, and therefore I do
not scold you for doubting my mettle, your own
being much softened no doubt by hardship and
suffering, Lord help you! But go back at once

to your ship, I prithee, and bid Master Wilkins look to his armament, be sober and prayer- ful, and hold himself ready to lay on to an enemy."

With this comfort I returned to the *Sea Lion*, and telling Captain Wilkins my fears and my uncle's decision, he lost no time in charging the guns and setting out muskets, swords, and brown bills ready to every man's hand. Like- wise he mustered the crew when all had been prepared, and gave them out a very good prayer, at the same time bidding the men trust to their own defence as well as the mercy of Providence (should we be presently attacked) and give no quarter. To this address would Sir Bartlemy have added a hearty "amen" had he been present, for it was just after his own sturdy heart.

The strange sail bore down to within half a mile of us, being a swifter ship than either of ours, and making way where we could none, etc.; and then she held off on a tack and came no nearer. And though she showed no guns, yet could we see she was a powerful ship, and such as, for the value of her, would not venture abroad in these troublesome times without good arms.

About noon the breeze grew stronger and more steady, and so continued that by sundown we had made in all twelve sea leagues. All this time had the strange sail followed in our wake, standing off never much over half a mile. Then Captain Wilkins and all on board were convinced that this was an enemy seeking to injure us, and it seemed that Sir Bartlemy was equally of our way of thinking, for by means of his signals he bade us double our watch, keep our lanterns well trimmed, and hold close to him. And this we did, no man taking off his clothes, but every one who lay down having his arms ready to his hand. For my own part, I quitted not the deck all that night; nor could I take my eyes from the lights on board the *Faithful Friend* two minutes together for thinking of the dear girl who lay there, and whose life and honour were in our keeping.

We could see no lights in our track at all
during the night, whereby we hoped that our
enemy—as I may call her—seeing not ours, had
fallen away in the darkness; but when day
broke we perceived her still following us, and
no further away than before, so that we knew she
had been guided by our lamps, and had lit none
of her own.   In short, not to weary the reader,
as she had followed us that night and the day
before, so she clung to our heels for four days
and nights after.   And now being off Portugal,
Sir Bartlemy might have run into port; but
this he would not do; for, firstly, the breeze
continued all this time fairly prosperous; and,
secondly, his bold and stubborn nature would
not permit him to swerve from his course, or
show fear of any one.

By this time our company began to murmur
because they got no proper rest through con-
stant watching, and because (though they feared
no mortal enemy) they began to look upon this
pursuing ship as a thing without substance—
an unearthly sign of impending destruction, a

device of the fiend—I know not what, for seamen are ever prodigiously superstitious and easily terrified by that which passes their comprehension; and it strengthened their dread that this ship was painted black from stem to stern. Indeed, to a mind reasonably free from superstition, there was something dreadful and terrific in this great black ship following us with so great a perseverance, which put me in mind of some carrion bird with steadfast patience hovering slowly about wanderers beleaguered in a desert, with some forecast that in the end one must fall to become its easy prey.

These six nights did I get no rest, but only a little dog-sleep in the day when my body yielded to the fatigue of watching, my mind being quite disordered with dreadful apprehensions; for well I knew that if by storm we got separated in the day, or by accident of fog or such like lost each other in the night, then would our enemy fall upon us one after the other, and overcome us; which, though we fought like lions, might well arrive, seeing she

M

was so much bigger than either of us, and manned with a greater company, as I could descry through a perspective. My own life I valued not; my fear was all lest Lady Biddy should fall a prey into the wicked hands of that bloody, subtile Rodrigues. What could that dear, sweet creature do to resist him? What fate would be hers, being at his mercy? These questions did provoke fearful answers in my anxious imagination, to my inexpressible torment.

At length, on the seventh day, we being then, as Captain Wilkins told me, off the coast of Morocco, and the wind falling to a calm, I took a boat and rowed to my uncle's ship. And when I got aboard I found the company there in not much better case than ours on the *Sea Lion*, for every man had a sullen and unhappy look on his face, and from time to time cast his eye towards the black ship that lay behind us, for all my uncle pacing the deck did rate them most soundly for not going quicker about the business he set them; swearing at them like a heathen Jew, so that one, not knowing his kind and generous heart, had thought him a very tyrant.

My first thought was of Lady Biddy, and casting my eye up and down the deck to see if her fair face and dainty figure were there, my limbs shook and my teeth chattered together with the intensity of my desire. But she was nowhere visible.

" Well, Benet, what the plague has brought you from your ship ? " asks my uncle, roughly, as he comes to my side. " What do you fear, that you are spying up and down, your cheeks pale, and your lips on a quiver ? "

" Lady Biddy," says I, with a thickness in my voice, " is she well ? "

" Ay, and if all on this ship were as stout of heart I should have more reason to be grateful," says he.

" Thank God she is well! May no mischance befall her! " says I, in a low tone.

" And what mischance may befall her if we act like men in her defence ? "

M 2

I cast my eyes towards the black ship, and then said I to my uncle—

"Rodrigues is there, I know."

"You shall lend me your spyglass, for I think you have seen him, to be so cock-sure."

"No, sir, I have not seen him; but I am sure he commands that ship. A painter is known by his workmanship."

"I know nothing of painting and such fiddle-faddle. Speak straight to the purpose, man," says my uncle, with a curse.

"Well," says I, "no man but Rodrigues could devise such subtle, devilish means for our destruction."

"In this holding on yet holding off, I see nothing but the device of a fool or a coward, be he Rodrigues or another."

"He is neither a fool nor a coward," says I; "he values his ship and his men too high to attack us at a disadvantage. He knows, as well as you do, that this patient following, while it muses his company and rests them, is fatiguing ours, and sapping the foundation of their courage."

" I warrant their courage will return to the dogs with the first shot that is fired."

" Then may it be too late ; for, you may be sure of this, Rodrigues will not fire a ball until he is sure of our defeat," says I.

" Sure of our defeat! And pray when may that be?" asks he, firing up with disdain.

" When accident helps him either to fall in with his comrade Parsons, or by our getting sundered through some mishap. He has as many men on his ship (as you may plainly see) as we have in both our companies, and more. How are we to combat him singly?"

" Why, with God's help and our own good arms," says he, sternly ; but the moment after that he turned his eyes towards the black ship, measuring it ; and his silence proclaimed that he could not overlook his peril. Presently, in a more subdued tone, he says, " Well, nephew, I doubt not you had some better intention than to damp my spirits in coming here, so if you would offer any advice, out with it, for the love of God, and I promise I will listen with as much patience and forbearance as I may command."

"Sir," says I, "you are making for the Canaries, and there, in all likelihood, is Parsons, awaiting the coming of his confederate, so that we are, as it were, going before the tiger into the lair of his mate." My uncle nodded acquiescence. "Now, if I might advise, I would have you alter your course, and make for the Windward Isles, and so down to Guiana. Then, if Rodrigues does also alter his course, I should draw upon him, and seek so to disable him with a shot amidst his masts as he should be disabled from following us further."

"Now, indeed, do you talk good sense, and such as is after my heart," cries he, joyfully. "This will I do at once; so go you back and bid Wilkins prepare to shape his course this way."

But seeing that I yet lingered, as loth to depart, he claps me on the shoulder and says, "What else would you have, Benet?"

"Why, sir," says I, "I would have you send another with your message, and suffer me to stay here in his place."

"Why, are you so weak-kneed as that?" says he. "Well, 'tis in the nature of mice to be timorous; but I looked for better stuff in a man of our family."

"Nay," says I; "if I feared Rodrigues I should not ask to stay here, for 'tis this ship he will attack, knowing, as he must, by our sailing, that our general and leader is here."

"Why, that is true," says he; and then he fell into a silence, and looked at me keenly to divine why I wished to stay there. After a little while, marking the hot blood in my face, and knowing it was to be near Lady Biddy that I sought this change of ships, he put his hands on my shoulders, and says he, very kindly, and with a little trembling of pity in his voice, "My poor Benet, the best thing you can do for her sake is to go back to your ship and stay not in this. Ay, and for your own sake it were better too. The enemy you

have to overcome is the passion in your own
breast, which is more capable to bring ruin to
your soul and sorrow to our hearts than are the
guns of Rodrigues to endanger our bodies. Go
back, dear fellow."

And knowing how this passion had before,
by its hopelessness, brought me into evil ways
and despair of better, I accepted his guidance,
and went back to my ship, though with a sore
heart.

And going back I saw my lady standing in
the stern gallery of the *Faithful Friend*. But
she did not see me, or, seeing me, made no sign;
for why should she trouble to descry whether it
were I or another sitting there? And clasping
my hands together I prayed God (within myself)
to dispose of her to her own happiness and His
praise.

CHAPTER XV.

WE FALL INTO SORE DISASTERS OF RAGING TEMPEST AND BLOODY BATTLE.

As soon as I was got on board I told Captain Wilkins of our generalissimo's intention, which he heard with much satisfaction, and did straightway communicate with his crew, who thereupon set up a great cheer. About two o'clock, the breeze freshening, the *Faithful Friend* changed her course and we with her, and for two hours we ran west, though the wind had been more prosperous for making south. Yet did the black ship follow us in this course persistently as in the other, keeping always the same distance in our wake. Then did Sir Bartlemy signal us to open all our ports for the guns to play, and to stand every man to his post, which we did very cheerfully and as smartly as ever the company on the *Faithful*

Friend did.   And though this preparation might
well be seen from the black ship, we could see
with our perspectives no such preparation on
her, so that the simple would have conceived
she had no lower ports for guns, and was an
unarmed trader.   Then Sir Bartlemy signalled
us to stand-to, yet to be in readiness to come to
his help if need arose, which we did; meanwhile
he puts about and sails down on the black
ship, who kept her ports closed, but stayed
his coming patiently.

Being come within speaking distance, Sir
Bartlemy takes his speaking horn and spreads
out his ancient; whereupon the black ship
spread hers, which was true English, and every
way as good as ours.   Then our general through
his horn demanded what ship that was and why
she did so persistently dog us.   To this a man
from the black ship replied that she was the
Robin Goodfellow, of Southampton, commanded
by Richard Simons, and a very peaceable trader,
bound for Campeachy Bay to barter for dye-
wood, and that she meant us no harm, but only

sought to have protection against pirates by sailing in the company of two ships so well armed as we.

"Then," shouts my uncle, "be you like your ship, a good fellow, and sheer off, for we like your room better than your company; and sheer off at once [adds he] or I will pepper your jacket to a pretty tune."

To show he meant to be as good as his word, he bade his gunner fire a broadside wide of the black ship, which did the gunner very faithfully, hurting no one. "Though, would to God!" says my uncle, afterwards, "I had been wise enough to fire amongst his rigging for a better earnest."

The black ship made no response; but, turning about, held off before the wind half a mile and no more; and my uncle, sailing upon her to make her go to a greater distance, she sheered off, keeping always the same distance; and this manœuvre was repeated twice or thrice till Sir Bartlemy, guessing she was endeavouring to lure him away from us, and seeing it

was useless to try and come up to close quarters
with a ship that could sail two furlongs to his
one, gave up this attempt and rejoined us. Our
captain tried to make his men believe that the
black ship was what her captain represented,
and that he, in still following us—which he
did as though he had received no warning, or
scorned to accept it—was merely showing a
stubborn spirit and not a hostile one, since he
had not showed any guns or fired in defiance to
us. Some of our better men accepted this; but
there were many who could not stomach it, and
openly cursed the day when they had come to
sea on this venture.

So held we on, and my uncle, hoping the
black ship would have to stay for water and
refreshment at the Azores (for we had gone
from our course that if the black ship were
indeed bound for Campeachy she might have
no further pretext to hang on our heels), and
being himself still very well victualled, would
not stay there, but, passing them, bore down
towards the Bermuthes; but neither would the

black ship stay there, but kept to our heels as perversely as ever.

Now, being come to the Bermuthes, that befell which I feared, for the seas, which are greatly troubled at those parts, rose prodigiously, and with it there came a most terrible hurricano, which obliged us to run with a single small sail. This gale did so buffet and hurl us about as we could with much pain keep to our course and reasonably near our consort during the day; but at night it was worse, for no lanterns of ours could be kept burning, nor was any of the *Faithful Friend's* to be seen, and though from time to time we fired off our petereros for a signal, yet answer heard we none for the raging of the sea. In this terrible tempest we were sorely bruised, our little sail split to shreds, and no chance to rig another, so that we tossed helpless on the water, expecting every moment to founder. But it pleased God to spare us this time.

I shall not dwell on the horrors of that night, nor of the next day, and the night following, but come briefly to the morning of the third day of our tribulation, when, by help of such sail as we could set, we drifted out of that horrid region and came into calmer waters; in which time we had been swept an incredible distance; but, lord! so broken in our masts, riggings, and elsewhere as it was pitiable to see; besides three men short of our number, who we counted were washed away in that hurricano. Then looking around could we see nothing of the *Faithful Friend*, nor of the black ship neither; so that we reckoned one or both had gone to the bottom.

To think that Lady Biddy was no more affected me so grievously that I threw myself on the deck, not caring what became of me, and lamenting that I lay not at the bottom of that cruel sea with her. But Captain Wilkins kept a brave heart (God be praised!), and, hoping yet to see our consort again, contrived to set up some sort of sails, fresh rig his rudder, and restore order on board, so that ere long we were making good way towards Trinidado (as we judged), where it had been agreed we should

in case of separation seek rendezvous. On the
morning of the fourth day, ere yet there was
full daylight, but only twilight, as I was standing on the poop deck very melancholy and
dejected, I heard the sound of guns to the south
of the course we were making; and Captain
Wilkins, to whom I ran in all speed to communicate these tidings, did likewise believe he
heard this sound; whereupon he at once shaped
our course in that direction, whereby in a little
time we were further assured that these sounds
were real, and not bred of imagination. The
reports were not apart, like signals, but con-
tinuous; so that we knew it was the can-
nonading of ships in battle, which stirred every
man to make all haste; and indeed we did all
we could think on to speed our ship; still were
we slow, for our want of sail, which made us
furious with impatience.

There was a haze upon the water, so that
when the tumult of guns was loud in our ears,
we could see nothing; but now the sun getting up strong over the horizon and sucking up

the mist, we of a sudden caught sight of the
flashing guns, and then of a ship not many
furlongs off, broadside towards us, which we
presently descried to be the black ship; though
now her whole side was open with ports, from
which her guns shone out like teeth. At the
same time we perceived that she was grappled
on stem and stern to another ship on the further
side, which we doubted not was the *Faithful
Friend;* upon which we did all set up a prodigious cheer; and Captain Wilkins putting
about, we passed the black ship at less than a
furlong distance, and dealt into her the whole
weight of our great guns on that side without
getting a single shot in return. The reason of
this was that all that ship's company were
occupied on the other side plying their cannon
and boarding the *Faithful Friend* (which we
recognised in nearing the black ship), as was
evident from the rattle of muskets and small
arms between the peals of the great guns.

But after getting this dose from us, they
were not long in manning their guns on the

hither side, as we found to our cost when, putting about once more, we sailed down to give him the other broadside; for their cannon belched out with such fury as laid many a stout seaman between our decks low, besides shooting away our rudder, which rendered us helpless, as it were.

Seeing this, I begged Captain Wilkins to give me a boat and such of his men as could be spared to go and succour our friends, to which he agreed readily enough, and forthwith lowered our barge; whereupon I, with a score of hearty fellows, all armed to the teeth, sprang in, and rowed with all our might to that side of the grappled ships where lay the *Faithful Friend*. Through one of her lower ports we scrambled, one after the other, but I the first, you may be sure; and there it was all thick with stinking gunpowder smoke, and strewn with dead men, and such as were too sorely wounded to join in the battle above, and no man ever heard greater din than there was of big guns and small, the clashing of steel, the

N

trampling on the decks, the shouting and cursing of men fighting, and the sad groaning of
the hurt, and such confusion as you could not
tell one sound from another scarcely.

This did but spur us on to be doing, and
like so many cats we sprang up through the
hatchways by the ladders, and so came on the
main deck, taking no heed of the poor fellows
who lay heaped at the foot of those ladders,
nor of the blood that trickled in thick drops
from step to step, splashing in our faces as if
it had been mere rain water, and lay smeared
down the handrails, where many a good man
had pressed his bleeding body for support.

Now, as I sprang on deck, did I find myself
in the very midst and thick of these wicked
pirates, who were readily to be distinguished
from honest seamen by the red skirts which
they wear who bind themselves to the regulations of their Order.

Just before me was a culverdine pointed
against the roundhouse, into which the crew of
the *Faithful Friend* (such as were not laid low)

had retired, and were there barricadoed, and a
fellow stood over against it, blowing his match
to fire the piece. And this man I knew full
well for a villain of the old *Sure Hawk's* company, and with the axe in my hand I struck
him between the teeth right through to his
neck-joint. He was the first man I had ever
slain; but I counted it as nothing, being
wrought to very madness with passion, and
wrenching my axe from his bone, I turned upon
another rascal who was making at my side with
his knife, and with a back-handed blow, the
hinder part of my weapon crashed his forehead
into his brains as you might with your thumb
break the shell of an egg into the yolk. By
this time my good comrades had sprung up
behind me to my help, else had my fight soon
come to an end; for the pirates, getting over
the amazement into which my sudden attack
had thrown them, with a shout of rage turned
all upon me.   Then did we so lay about us that
we beat the pirates back into the fore part of the
ship, and truly I do think that if those of our

N 2

friends in the roundhouse could then have come to our help we should have won the day; but, as ill-luck would have it, they had taken such pains to barricado themselves, to prevent the pirates coming at them, that they could not immediately get out to get at their foes, and so, for want of support, were we undone. For there were of the pirates two score, I take it, and more coming to their succour over the side every moment, while we, not counting those who may have fallen, were but one score, all told.

Foremost among our enemies was Rodrigues himself, who did look a very devil for rage, with the grime of smoke and blood about his face, his white, pointed tusks bared to the gums, and his eyes flaming with fury. His head was bound about with a bloody clout, for he had got a wound, and through the grime of powder-smoke on his face there was a bright channel where he blood still wept. But for all his wounds he fought better and more desperately than any of the rest; and seeing that those in the roundhouse were struggling to get out to our help, and that his only chance lay in beating us down ere they succeeded, he threw himself forward with nothing but a long curved knife in his hands. His intention was to settle my business, seeing that I had done him this mischief; and surely he would have achieved it (for I was closely grappled with a fellow, my arms about him and his about me, each seeking to get freedom for the use of the knives in our hands), but that a comrade, seeing my peril, dealt at him with his brown bill, driving the spike into his shoulder. On this, Rodrigues, with a howl of rage, struck out the point from his shoulder, and turning on this poor man with his hooked knife ripped him up from the navel as you might a rabbit. At that moment I threw my man on his back, and in falling on the deck my knife was driven up to the hilt through his loins. Then did I get a terrible blow on the head (from whom I know not), so that I lost all consciousness, and lay like one dead.

CHAPTER XVI.

Now must I speak of what happened on board the *Faithful Friend* after my discomfiture; not from my own knowledge—for knowledge had I none, being felled, as I say, like an ox—but from what I afterwards learnt from others.

Headed by Rodrigues, the pirates cleaved our little company in two, and so surrounded them with great numbers that their case was hopeless, and in short time they were beaten down every man, and left for dead, these heartless pirates giving no quarter to any. And while these few were being despatched, Rodrigues, with a following of shouting fiends, returned to attack those who were making their way out of the roundhouse, and by the fury of that onslaught did they cut down all those who had got out, and forced them within once more to set up their barricadoes.

Then, seeing no further danger on board the *Faithful Friend* but such as a round dozen of his rogues might cope with, he called off the rest to return on board his ship to defend it against the *Sea Lion*. For Captain Wilkins, having set out two long sweeps or galley oars from the lower stern gallery to serve as a rudder, had returned to the attack, and coming cheek by jowl with the black ship, he grappled her in his turn, so that now all three ships were bound together, and thus, with their cannons mouth to mouth did they discharge their shot one into the other with incredible bitterness.

But here the black ship being but poorly manned—most of her company being on the *Faithful Friend*—played but the weaker part; seeing which, Master Wilkins resolved to board her with his men, and so make his way over her decks to the deliverance of his consort. He called his men to clamber the sides of the black ship and escalade her bulwarks. But against

such an attack was the black ship well provided,
for not only were her bulwarks at arms' length
above those of the *Sea Lion*, but furnished with
a devilish device of broken sword blades, spikes,
and sharp nails set in long spars and lashed to
the side, so that nowhere could a man make
headway, or surmount without cruel gashes.
While the poor brave men were beating down
this defence, Rodrigues and his wretches came
pouring back to the defence of the black ship,
and while some mowed down the attackers from
their high bulwarks with axe and sword, other
some were sent below to recruit their fellows at
the big guns.   Rodrigues himself did direct
these pieces, so bending down their mouths that
the shot should go through the decks to beat out
the side below water.   And so well did he thrive
in this wickedness that presently, after these
great guns had been fired, the *Sea Lion* began
to fill, and the men on board, seeing they must
perish by drowning if they stayed in her, for-
sook their pieces, and, rushing all on deck, cast
aside their arms, fell on their knees, and begged

mercy of Rodrigues. And let it not be thought they were cowards for this, but put yourself in their place, and consider if the fear of death would not have moved you to the same distress.

Rodrigues, not wishing to lose all the *Sea Lion* contained, removed his defence of sword blades, etc., and bade the men come up, which they did, all save Captain Wilkins, who, with his sword in his hand, stood alone on the deck. Rodrigues, taking a musket in his hand, bade this brave man lay down his sword or die; but he took no notice of this command, whereupon did Rodrigues level his piece and shot him dead where he stood.

Then Rodrigues sent down a parcel of his men to staunch the leak in the side of the *Sea Lion*, and this they did by lowering a leaded sail upon the outer side to cover the holes; after which the water was pumped out and the carpenters repaired the breach more securely, so that there was no further peril of her going down.

And now being masters of both ships, the pirates made great rejoicing, for though there were yet those in the roundhouse of the *Faithful Friend* who were unfettered, yet were they close prisoners and powerless to recover their ship, or do mischief, except in foolhardy desperation, to their captors.

To every pirate was dealt out double allowance of meat and drink, but the latter not of a strong kind, for Rodrigues knew full well that a drunken bout might prove their undoing. As for the prisoners, they got naught to eat, but only jeers and derision.

While his men were yet carousing, Rodrigues goes on the poop deck of the *Faithful Friend*, and stamping his heel to call attention of those below, he cried out to know if Sir Bartlemy Pengilly was yet alive; to which Sir Bartlemy himself replied—

"Ay," says he, "and I hope to live yet to see you hanged, villain!"

"Well," replies the other, "you'll not get that chance unless you accept my conditions."

"I will make no conditions with such as you," cries my uncle.

"You had better, my friend," says Rodrigues jeeringly; "'twill save you a deal of trouble in the long run."

To this my uncle made no reply but one of his sea oaths.

"I shall leave you to the better guidance of your company," says Rodrigues, "who, I have no doubt, will bring you to reason when they begin to feel the pinch of starvation. But, mark this, if you hurt only by accident a single hair of my men with the arms you hold so precious, I will cannonade you where you are, and spare not one single life."

Then calling to his boatswain he bade him whistle his company to their posts, and pointing to the deck, all hampered with dead and dying men, he cried—

"Look to your comrades; let not one of your fellows who has a spark of life escape your care. For the other carrion, fling it overboard, no matter whether it be dead or living."

These words I heard, for at that moment I was waking from my trance.

CHAPTER XVII.

I AM SHOT OUT OF ONE SHIP AND CRAWL INTO ANOTHER, WITH WHAT ADVANTAGE MAY YET BE SEEN.

My first feeling on recovering consciousness was of a great weight oppressing me, and this I presently found was due to two dead men lying athwart me, where they had fallen in their last agony. Using all my strength, it was as much as I could do to thrust them off—one fellow lying across my breast with his shoulder against my throat, and the other again across my middle, his arms thrown out upon the first.

The cause of my weakness was not that blow that had felled me, but the loss of blood from two wounds—one in my thigh and the other in the thick of my arm—which I had received without any knowledge on my part, and now for the first time discovered by my clothes being.

glued to those parts and a great smarting when I struggled to free myself from the weight of the dead bodies.

Being once more able to breathe freely, I lay back on the deck exhausted and faint with the effort, and slowly brought back to my mind what had happened. The silence on board, save for the sound of revelling from the black ship alongside, told me that the battle was over ; and it needed but little to convince me how the fight had ended ; but, thinking of my dear Lady Biddy, I presently set my hands, all stiff and sticky with blood, on the deck, and raised myself up, looking towards the coach.   Then it was I saw Rodrigues and heard him order his men to cast all us poor fellows, whom he termed carrion, overboard, without regard to our being dead or living.   Then, once more, a weariness as of death coming over me, I fell again on my back, with a giddiness in my head and despair at heart, which robbed me of all vigour, while the stench of spilled blood made my bowels heave with sickness.   The pirates, coming now to clear the deck, took up one poor corpse, lifted him on to the bulwarks, and so bundled him over; and in this wise three or four more, when, seeing the labour before them, one fetched from below a wooden gangway wherewith they slide merchandise from a wharf down into the ship, which they now thrust through one of the upper deck gun ports, making it fast with cords. This way, with less trouble and much quicker, they shot the " carrion " into the water, taking no heed if some poor wretch but slightly wounded did cry for pity and mercy, except by inhuman laughter and fiendish jests.

Two or three rascals came and carried off the corpses I had thrust from me, and then I knew my turn was come, and naught could save me, for I had no strength to help myself. And back came those two (who were new hands and so did not recognise me), and one kicking me over on my face, the other took up my legs by the knees, while the first laid hold of me by the shoulders, and so they bore me, like so much butcher's flesh to the cutting board, and flung

me on to the slanting gangway. By this time
the slope was all slippery with gore of blood, so
that no sooner was I cast on than I slid down
like a stone, and shot thence deep into the
sea below.

Now, whether I owed it to the cold, in-
vigorating virtue of the refreshing sea, the
smarting anew of my wounds in the salt thereof,
or the instinct which possesses nearly every
creature to make one final struggle for existence
in the presence of death, I cannot say; only this
I know that no sooner had the waters closed
over my head than energy returned to my spirit
and strength to my limbs, and striking out
manfully with my arms and legs, I shortly came
to the surface of the water, not more than a
couple of fathoms from the stern of the *Faithful
Friend*.

But here was no hold at all, nor could I see
that I was much better off than if I had never
risen from the deep, till, casting my eyes about,
I spied a rope hanging over the stern of the
black ship and trailing in the sea, which rope

was part of her rigging (for she also had suffered
in the gale, to say nothing of our shot). To
this I swam, and being still full of my new-born
vigour, I drew on it till it became taut, and I
could keep my head above water with no
exertion at all.

Here I rested a bit, all the while searching
how I might better my condition, and perceiving
that my rope passed over the lower stern gallery,
I presently got the rope betwixt my knees, and
by passing one hand over the other made a shift
to pull myself up, though not without difficulty,
for as I drew myself out of the water I began
to turn round and round on the strained rope
like a joint of meat at the end of a string.
However, this was but a trifle of trouble, and
hand over hand I climbed up till at length I
reached the gallery, where I took another rest,
and returned thanks to God with as grateful a
heart as I could find.

This gallery, I take it, opened into the
steward's room, for through the ports I heard
the clinking of mugs and the voices of men

within, and seeing that at any moment some
fellow might look out and spy me, I felt it
would not do to linger there; so I went again
to my rope, which hung conveniently on one
side of the ports, and pulled myself up to the
gallery above, which is what is called the captain's parade, that balcony against the chief
cabins where the officers alone are privileged to
walk.   Here, as luck would have it, the wreck
of a sail hanging down from the deck above
formed a kind of screen, where I might rest for
the present secure from observation.   With a
glad heart I crawled under this refuge, and,
sitting down to fetch my breath, I thought it
not amiss to look to my wounds.   On the crown
of my head was a lump as big as a fair egg, and
the scalp cut, but no longer bleeding; in my thigh
was a pike wound about three inches long, but
not deep.   By tearing off the foot of my stocking
and so drawing the other part high, I managed
to make a very fair dressing for this wound.
The other, which was, as I say, in the fleshy
part of my arm, gave me but little anxiety, for,

o

though it still bled pretty freely, I could get at
it easily, and, binding it round with my necker-
chief, I felt no further concern about it, but
only satisfaction to find that my case was no
worse.

Scarcely had I come to this conclusion
when I heard the trampling of feet on the
deck above, and the sound of voices, with one
in a higher tone giving orders. And the first
thing these men did was to haul upon the sail
which screened me.

"I am a lost man if I stay here longer,"
thinks I; so slipping along still under the
sail I came to the little door opening on to
the gallery. By happy chance this was not
fastened, save by a latch, and seeing, as I
peered through the lattice window, that no one
was on the other side, I slipped through, and
found myself in a prodigious fine cabin; for this
Rodrigues was no common, sluttish jack-sailor,
but a man who, when he could afford it, lived
like any prince, indulging himself in every
extravagant luxury that a voluptuous taste

can conceive. Here was a thick carpet on
the floor, and all round the sides ran a sofett,
furnished with cushions in the Moors' style.
with fine paintings and mirrors above, and
a lantern of coloured glass like gems hanging
from the ceiling, which was painted as pretty
as could be with devices of flowers and cherubs.
To the windows were silk curtains of a rose
colour; but to speak of all these appointments
have I no time; only will I say this that
never anywhere else have I seen such expense
wasted as in the cabin of this scoundrel pirate.
Nor had I time or inclination then to take
note of all this bravery, being only concerned
to find me some hole where I might hide for
safety. And now came a bustle on the outside of the cabin, so that I felt I had but
come out of the fryingpan into the fire, and
which way to turn I knew not. I could not
go into the body of the ship for the men
there, nor back into the gallery neither for
the men above; yet to stay where I stood
would be as bad as either.

o 2

In this pickle I halted till spying an
opening on one side between the sofetts, I
pushed the gilded panel to see if, perchance,
this were some fantastic kind of door; and,
sure enough, it was, giving way readily to
my hand, and closing behind me softly with
spring-work.   And there I found myself in
a cabin smaller than the other, but still mighty
fine, and fitted up as a bed chamber, with a
good cot fixed on one side, hung with saffron
taffety.   Other door to this chamber was
there none; nor could I see any place of
safety but under the cot, whither therefore I
did creep — recommending myself to Providence — without further ado, and not a whit
too soon neither, for scarcely had I got my
long legs well out of sight when the door
opened and a boy came in, as I could see by
his little bare feet peeping under the valance.

Putting my eye close to the ground, I saw
him go to a polished chest on the other side
and fetch from one drawer a clean shirt and
a pair of stockings; then from another slop-

shoes, a pair of trunks, and the like; till, having set out all that was necessary, he gathered them up in his arms and carried them away, from which I opined that Rodrigues had yet another cabin where he was about to change his bloody and besmirched clothes for these other. Nor was I far out in this surmise, for in some ten minutes or so the door was flung open, and I caught sight of those same slop-shoes and clean stockings for a moment as he stood by the side of the cot thrusting back the curtains before he threw himself down to rest. As his deep breathing proclaimed that he had fallen asleep, I was for a while sorely tempted to creep out from my hiding-place and cut the villain's throat as he lay there; nay, so well could I make out where he lay over my head that, putting the point of my jack-knife against the sacking, I felt sure that I could, with one forcible thrust, drive it up into his black heart. Yet I could not do this either way; for, first, my sentiment revolted against taking the life of a defenceless man, as against murder—despite his cruel treatment of the helpless wounded and myself—and then my reason forbade me to attempt such a desperate measure, for if Rodrigues died, there yet remained forty or fifty desperate villains to overcome, and how was one wounded man by any possibility to accomplish that feat? To fail in such an attempt would be to provoke the enemy to such a fury of revenge that he would massacre every one of those whose release had been attempted. I say massacre, but a yet worse fate might be reserved for Lady Biddy, whose dear sake now did most concern me. With this reflection I gently shut up my jack-knife, and slipped it back into my pocket for better employment.

CHAPTER XVIII.

THE bumping and grinding together of the ships had ceased before Rodrigues came to take rest, showing that the grapnels were cast off that bound the three ships together; and now, from the easy movement, I surmised that we were under way, and making for some haven for the greater convenience of repairing injuries, distributing of stores, refreshment, etc., which was indeed the case. On board the *Sea Lion* Rodrigues had set a sufficiency of men to work her, and on the *Faithful Friend* a greater number for a like purpose, and to serve as guard over the prisoners in the roundhouse, while the rest he took with him on board his own ship to lead the way and conduct the prizes he had taken. About eight o'clock that evening (as I judge) we seemed to have come into very smooth water, and then the boy coming to the cabin called to Rodrigues that the master did wish to speak to him; whereupon Rodrigues sprang up and went out. Then for the first time could I stretch my limbs with ease; for though the bustle on deck, the hammering of the carpenters, and such noisy business affected his slumbers not in the least, yet did I but turn upon the carpet under his cot, his breathing would show that the sound had alarmed his senses, which was a remarkable thing, but not without parallel, for those who live in peril develop, as I may say, a new sense which never sleeps. Thus had I been constrained to lie very still (which was doubtless of great advantage to me for the healing of my wounds, but very little to the repose of my bones), for I knew full well that had he found me under his cot he would have slain me there, helpless as I was for defence, without any such compunction as stayed my hand from taking his life.

So now, as I say, being free to move, I

stretched myself and turned me about with great relief and satisfaction, for here, as I take it, had I been lying on my back without motion the best part of ten hours. Presently I heard the voice of Rodrigues on the deck above, and feeling mighty faint for want of food, I lifted the valance and peeped out. There was just light enough to descry a wine cooler in the corner of the cabin over against the chest I have mentioned, and urged on by my necessity I made bold to wriggle out from my hiding-place and creep over to it. By good chance it was unlocked, and inside were half a dozen good bottles, of which I scrupled not to appropriate the first I laid my hand on; then to make a good job of it while I was about it, I pried into a cabinet hard by, where by another good chance I lighted on a dish of dried raisins. Well content with this booty, I hied me back under the cot, and rolling up a corner of the carpet to serve as a pillow, I managed to refresh myself to my heart's content. Nay, I think I drank more of that wine (the most excellent that ever

I did taste) than was good, for despite my
determination to keep awake, I unconsciously
fell asleep, which was the maddest thing a
man in his right senses could have done; for
had Rodrigues come back into that cabin he
would surely have discovered me by my hard
breathing; but this (thanks be to God!) he did
not do; for having rested himself, he gave permission to his crew to relax awhile likewise,
himself going on board the *Faithful Friend* for
the better custody of the prisoners there, as I
believe.

At this time the three ships, brought all
well together, lay anchored within a good bay
(as I am told) in an island which I take it
must have been one of the Bahamas.

I was awoke by a bustling in the next cabin,
to find the sun streaming full under the edge
of the cot valance. I heard Rodrigues speaking
there in a tone of command, but what he said
my senses were yet too confused to make out;
then I caught sight of the 'boy's feet again
as he entered that one where I lay and set

something down. And now he comes very briskly to the cot and sets about stripping it; that done, he shakes up the bed, turns it over as any maid would, and fetches out from the chest clean sheets, which he lays in the place of those he had stripped off, and so makes up the bed; after which he sets the furniture in order, and, tucking the foul linen under his arm, goes out. '

All this while there was prodigious hurrying to and fro over head, tumbling of heavy goods below, creaking of pulleys, shouting of orders, and like confusion, which was caused by the shipping aboard of the black ship all the stores and treasure belonging to the *Sea Lion* and the *Faithful Friend*, to which this rogue Rodrigues had a fancy. But to think that in the midst of all this pother he took heed to having clean sheets laid in his bed did astonish me beyond all things.

The bustle continued all the morning; once or twice the boy came in with parcels, which he set atop of that he had already brought, but

nothing else occurred to disturb my medita-
tions. And these, as I grew accustomed to
the noise around me, were of a very melancholy sort, not because of the sad outlook
concerning my own fortunes, for I may truly
say I had grown in a sort callous and indifferent to what became of me, but for thinking of Lady Biddy. I took myself very
grievously to task for having slept all through
that night like a log while she was in such an
extremity.

"Is this your devotion, wretch!" says I
to myself—"is this your love, that you can
slumber in peace while she, hived up with
rude sailors, destitute of common necessaries,
is in peril of death at the hands of her wicked
persecutors? Have you no bowels of pity,
that you could make not one effort to save
her, rascal?"

In this way I taunted myself, until, falling
into a more reasonable state of mind, I began to
reason as to what I might yet do in her behalf.
I concluded from the shifting of the stores that

Rodrigues had determined to abandon the two ships with their crew, for the mere hulls could be of little value to him. Coming to this decision, I was for getting away from the black ship and rejoining the *Faithful Friend*, that I might be near my Lady Biddy; but what could I then do? Was not this rather a gratification of my own selfish desire than a means of benefiting her? Was I not simply adding another hungry mouth to that destitute company? With these and a hundred such fruitless arguments did I torment myself; now preparing myself to get away, now resigning myself to stay where I was, getting no nearer to a rational determination in the end than I was in the beginning.

I was still in this torment when I heard the anchor weighing and the men singing as they are used to do at this business. Suddenly their singing ceased, and I heard a great angry clamour of voices from a distance; nay, I do think I heard my uncle's big voice above the rest, and then the fellows above replying with

laughter and derision, so that I knew we were
leaving that unhappy company behind, as was
the more evident by the bending of the ship
before the wind. Then, desperate to think I
was being carried away from Lady Biddy, I
took resolution to dash through the cabin to
the gallery and cast myself into the sea, and
to this end I had set my hands and feet against
the wall, to thrust my body from under the cot,
when the door was thrown violently open, the
cabin entered, and the sacking of the bed was
pressed down over my head, which made me
think that Rodrigues had come again to rest
himself.

Turning silently on to my back I glanced
under the valance. At a little distance were
the bare feet of the boy ; close to the valance,
standing beside the cot, were the feet of a man.
Thus they stood immovable for a space,
and then lightly they moved away and the
door was closed behind them. But the sacking above still bulged downwards with the
weight thrown on the bed. " Had Rodrigues

laid there a wounded comrade?" I asked myself.

That it was Rodrigues who had entered and left this cabin I was sure, for I now heard his voice speaking low, as if giving orders to the boy, in the one adjoining.

If it be a wounded comrade he has laid here, then is he badly hurt, thought I, as I lay with my eyes fixed on the sacking; for there was no sign of movement; nor was there any sound of groaning or the like.

Only for a few minutes did matters stand thus, however; then there was a little movement above, followed by a quick start, and the next instant, in the space below the valance, I saw descend the sweetest little foot that ever man did see, and then its fellow, both neatly shod, after which fell the hem of an envious petticoat that shut them from my sight.

My heart quite ceased to beat as I asked myself, "Who is this woman?"

For a moment she stood where she had stepped to the ground, as if looking around to realise where she was ; then like any doe she sprang towards the little windows that opened on to the gallery, and looking out, she gave a moan of despair, by which plaintive delicate sound I knew that this dear creature was Lady Biddy.

CHAPTER XIX.

Scarce had this piteous moan passed her tender lips when Rodrigues (as I am told), opening the door, made her a mighty respectful reverence, and, says he—

"Madam, I am delighted you have recovered of your swoon, and I trust you feel no ill-effect of the rough usage we were forced to exercise in bringing you hither."

"Where am I?" cries Lady Biddy fiercely. "Why have you brought me here?"

"You are on board the *Robin Goodfellow*," says he gravely, "or as my fellows prefer to call it, the *Black Death;* and I have brought you here because I had not the heart to leave you on the *Faithful Friend*, to endure the hardships to which her company must be reduced."

P

"Where is my uncle? Get you hence and bring him to me!" she cries, with the same impetuous fury.

"In anything else I shall obey you punctually," says he; "but it is impossible for me to comply with this demand, for Sir Bartlemy Pengilly is in the ship yonder, which we are leaving behind."

"You gave him your promise that not one of those who were in the roundhouse should be injured in any way if he laid down his arms. It was to save me from the violence of your crew that he submitted himself with the brave men who stood by him."

"Madam, it was to that very end I gave my promise. Undoubtedly, had your uncle stood out, I could not have stayed my company from firing into the roundhouse and putting an end to the obstinate resistance there, notwithstanding you were likely to have fallen a victim with your friends."

"Would to God we had met that fate, rather than trust to your promises, dastard villain!"

says she; "for then had there been an honour-
able end to their woes and mine."

"Patience, patience, lady!" says he, in a
tone calculated only to arouse her greater indignation. "You are much too young to die,
and too beautiful. Trust me, your fate will
be a happier one than you can at present conceive. When your spirits are calmer you will
see that this unfortunate business is due to
the impetuosity of your uncle, and that I am
the best friend you could have found, in the
midst of deplorable circumstances. Your uncle
fired the first shot, and the first man who fell
in the conflict was on board this ship. Could
you expect my men to see their innocent
comrades slaughtered with indifference, or me
to make no effort for their preservation from
further mischief? We fought, and having overcome those who would have overcome us, we
did all that a magnanimous victor could reasonably afford to do. We forgave those who laid
down their arms, and gave them a ship to
continue their journey in. I had promised no

P 2

injury should be inflicted upon you, and for
that reason I brought you hither, where, as
you see, you will be not ill-lodged, and shall
have the best nurture and service the stores
and my company can offer. Had I left you
on the *Faithful Friend* your case would have
been different, for the vessel is badly injured,
and I fear the company will be sorely put to
it for provisions, as, to supply our own wants,
we were obliged to take from her stores—a
poor recompense for the loss and injury inflicted upon us. I have been careful to have
your personal effects brought hither for your
use ; they are here. If anything is short of
your requirements, or if—— "

"Silence ! " cries Lady Biddy, who, turning
her back on Rodrigues, had tried to lend a
deaf, indifferent ear to his harangue, but was
at length by his long-winded perseverance and
mock-humility wrought to an intolerable degree
of impatience. "Silence ! " cries she, turning
upon him and stamping her little foot. "Leave
me, or, by my soul, I'll put an end to this

torment another way," and indeed (as I learn)
she did look around in desperation for some
instrument wherewith to destroy herself, being
very bitterly aggrieved by this hypocrite.

Again this Rodrigues makes her a low
reverence, and with his hand on the door says,
" I shall hope to find your spirits easier when
I next give myself the pleasure to inquire
after your condition. I have had refreshment
placed in this next cabin, and should you need
anything, you have but to pull the bell. And
so good-morning to your ladyship."

Lady Biddy gave him no reply, but as soon
as he had closed the second door after him—
turning the key in the outside, she ran to the
bed, and casting herself upon it, gave vent to her
feeling in an agony of tears.

And to hear her sobbing above me, yet
striving to smother the sound, lest Rodrigues
should know that her pride had broken down,
would have touched any stony heart. It was
so pitiful to my ear that the tears coursed down
my own cheeks as I listened.

Thus she sobbed in a great tumult for some while, and then her passion softening into mere maiden's sorrow, she murmured in a low tone, still smothering her sweet voice in the pillow lest it should be heard, and yet not able to keep quite silent neither—"Oh, my heart! Oh, my poor heart!" and this she said over and over again—"Oh, my poor heart! Oh, my heart!" with mournful tremor, unable to find other words to express the commotion of her feelings.

Now would I have given anything to be of comfort to her, yet I dared not come forth from where I lay, lest my sudden appearance should move her to cry out with terror ere she discerned who I was, which would have brought Rodrigues back in a twinkling, and ruined all. So I waited patiently awhile, and when she ceased to make moan, and only sobbed at intervals, like a child exhausted with weeping, I began to gently scratch the tick of the bed with my finger nail, making no more noise than might a mouse nibbling.

Of this she at first took no notice, but anon
I observed she smothered a sob, as if to listen
with greater attention, and then by the movement above I noticed she had started up as if
resting on her elbow; as I still continued the
scratching, she presently made a movement of
the clothes, as if to frighten the thing away, for
the bravest of women do greatly fear a mouse;
upon which, ceasing to scrape the tick, I said
quickly, in a very low whisper—

"Do not cry out, a friend is here—I, Benet
Pengilly!"

Then whipped she off the bed, yet making
no sound, and I, putting my hands and feet as I
have aforesaid against the wall, pushed myself
out from my cramped hiding-place, and got
upon my feet before her, raising my finger and
casting my eyes about for fear of discovery.

I must have been very villainous and horrid
to look upon, my hair untrimmed and hanging
about my face in dank wisps clotted with blood
from my wound, my clothes in a like pickle, and
no cleaner in my flesh than the sea had washed

me the day before; but such horrors had she
seen that her senses were, as it were, accustomed to dreadful images, and she saw me
no worse than others, but rather better, for
being there a friend where she thought was
none but enemies.

Catching the meaning of my gesture, she
went quickly to the panel door and spied into
the next cabin, whence she came back light of
foot, nodding to assure me all was safe.   Then
she gave me her hand, and I taking no heed
whether mine was reasonably clean or proper to
hold so dainty delicate a thing, took it; and to
feel those soft cool fingers clinging tightly to
my rough palm did seem to contract every
muscle of my back with physical delight.   Also
was my heart quickly moved with joy to perceive in her dear eyes — though they were
swollen and red with weeping—a bright beam
of hope and satisfaction, whilst the corners of
her lips curved with a little smile.

Coming quite close to me, she whispered
eagerly in my ear—

"You will save me, Benet, won't you?
You will be my good friend?"

"Ay," says I, as softly as she (if that might
be). "With God's help, no harm shall befall
you."

On this she presses my hand a little closer,
and then goes again to the door, from which
she returns with almost a child's glee to tell
me all is safe, and to ask by what miracle I
came to her succour.

This joy in the midst of such trouble and
peril, this kindness to me for whom she had
shown little liking hitherto, but rather detesta-
tion for the most part, will seem unnatural, as
being contrary to the proud high spirit and
independence of Lady Biddy, and so would it
have been at any other time; but there is none
—be he a man and never so strong—but grief
and terrible anxiety will reduce to the unresist-
ing soft temper of a child: so I do think and
thus explain this truth. And, indeed, she gave
present proof of weakness, for while the smile
was yet on her lips she clasps her hand to her

heart and sinks down, sitting on the bed as if
she could no longer hold her footing.

Seeing she was faint, I went with all speed
and reckless into the next chamber for that
refreshment Rodrigues said was set there for
her use—than which no madder thing fool ever
did, for there were windows opposite the gallery
looking on to the deck, and had one been prying
there I must have been seen, for all the two
curtains were drawn, there being space enough
for one to peep through from the outside if he
were so minded. But—thanks be to God!—
there was no one spying, and so I got the tray
of refreshments from the table where it lay and
carried it into the next cabin with no mischance.

This tray I set on the bed beside Lady
Biddy, and she ate and drank with appetite,
poor soul, for all the time they had been shut
up in the roundhouse—she, with her uncle, and
the poor remnant of his company—not one had
broken fast, for there was neither bit nor sup
to be got. Which also is a reason for that

behaviour of Lady Biddy's to which I have spoken as seeming unnatural.

While she satisfied her own cravings she made me eat likewise, whereto I was nowise loth myself, having eaten nothing for many hours but a few paltry raisins.

As she sat on the bed, I knelt on the ground by her feet for my better convenience in eating and also conversing in that low tone to which we were constrained. So as we ate I told her how I had come aboard and hidden myself, with other matters which there is no necessity to repeat; and this I did with reasonable calm, but the abounding joy and gladness of my heart to be there alone with that dear lady, kneeling at her very feet, listening to her whisper, feasting my eyes when hers were on the refreshment and I dared to do so unseen, no pen can describe, as I doubt also no imagination can conceive.

After she had eaten and drunk and would no more, being much refreshed and invigorated, I was for taking the tray back; but here her quick wit appearing where my dulness showed, she pointed out the danger, and taking the tray, carried it herself into the next chamber.

Coming back she seated herself on a settle that ran along one side of the cabin, and bidding me sit beside her, asked how I meant to contrive her escape, which indeed would have been a poser for me at another time, but did now to my excited imagination appear the easiest thing in the world. For when one's spirits are filled with joy there seems nothing insurmountable, as, on the other hand, in grief we can see no way out of our trouble.

"Why," says I, "we need not fear but we shall get away safe enough, and shortly too. For, as Rodrigues obligingly told you, the company is short of victuals, and must therefore lose no time in seeking a port where they can refresh with meat and drink ; besides that, the ship may need looking to for the damage she has got. And being in a port where there are Christian souls, what is to keep us here ? "

"A rascal named Rodrigues," says Lady Biddy, very pertinently.

"Pish!" says I. "I have escaped him times enough to know he is a fool, for all his pretence to cleverness. Nay, have I not hid myself under his own cot in broad day? Not dreaming but you are helpless, he will think you sufficiently secured if he locks the door and sets one of his rascals to watch it. But the stern gallery is open, and as I got in so can I get out, with the night to give me help and better security."

"Do you think it will be as easy for me?" asks Lady Biddy doubtfully.

"Ay, I shall make it so, please God," says I. "For in the night that I swim to shore will I bring back a boat, and by a ladder of ropes shall you get down into it."

Lady Biddy here nodded her head in hopeful approval.

"Once on shore we may hide ourselves safely, I do not question, and Rodrigues dare not waste a long time in looking for us, since the necessity that brought him hither will also bring on Sir Bartlemy. Then dare not these rascal pirates stay, lest they bring themselves to their well-earned gallows."

Then again Lady Biddy nodded to show her satisfaction, clasping her little hands at the same time, with a sigh in which all her trouble seemed to be wafted away. But in this moment of our confidence on future escape were we brought to consciousness of our present peril by the sudden opening of the door in the further chamber.

Together we started to our feet, and my first thought was to fetch the jack-knife from my pocket, but Lady Biddy, with that self-command which does animate women above men in the hour of danger to do the right thing and not the foolish one, quickly laid her hand on my arm to keep me still, and putting on as stern an air as any tragic player, went to the little betwixt door to ask Rodrigues why he dared disturb her.

But no Rodrigues was there; for it was

only the little blackguard boy he had sent in to know if madam would take a dish of chocolate.

When she had dismissed him, saying she needed no more to-day (it being now pretty nigh sundown, for I have bridged over many things), but would have her breakfast brought the next morning at seven, she came back to me, and we continued to talk of our escape, like any children of air castles, till the light faded.

And then with some trouble I began to see that I must presently go out of that chamber; and also I think Lady Biddy grew uneasy as to how I might conduct myself in the darkness of night, and she, so to speak, at my mercy.

Again the outer door opened; and this time the boy came to light the hanging lantern. She left the between door open when the lamp was lit and the boy again gone, and by a more cheerful bearing seemed to feel better at ease for this light.

"Presently," says I, "you will go in and put out that lamp."

"Why? Is it not more cheerful to have a light?" says she.

"Yes," says I, "but with that light burning I dare not go through the next cabin."

"Through it!" says she in wonder, and yet with a little fear in her tone; "whither are you going?"

"Out on the gallery," says I, "where I shall sleep very safely till the morning."

This would she not hear of, but would have me lie in her room while she reposed on the sofett in the next; that would I not allow, and so at length we compromised it in this wise: she kept her own chamber after putting out the lamp, and I, having bolted the door in the outer cabin, lay myself on the cushions there, she giving me her cloak that I might wrap it about me and so seem to be she if by accident she so overslept herself that she could not admit me to the inner chamber before daybreak.

And so with the cloak that she had worn on her dear body pressed to my lips I fell asleep that night a happier man than ever before I had been in all my life.

CHAPTER XX.

I SAY I fell asleep the happiest of men, with
sweet, delightful thoughts of that dear creature
who lay separated from me but by the thickness of a few panelled boards; yet were my
senses not so completely lulled to forgetfulness
but that they were quick to take alarm at that
which menaced her security, for suddenly I
awoke, hearing a sound at that door which
opened to the deck and which I had, as aforesaid, made fast on the inner side.

Sitting bolt upright I could see naught, for
the darkness was impenetrable; but it was
enough that I had ears to know some one was
trying the door. Slowly I heard the latch
grating as it was lifted in the catch, and then
the door creak as it was pressed from without;
but, thanks be to God, the bolt held firm.

Q

There was no light on the deck, or I should have caught some glimmer through the silk blinds of the windows; I could see no more than if I had been stone-blind. And the only other sound I heard was a sweeping down of rain upon the deck overhead. Presently the latch fell again, as my strained hearing could well perceive, and then there was a pause of some minutes, when again the latch was lifted slowly, and the door gave a smart crack under the pressure against it.

At the first sound I had started to my feet and opened my jack-knife; and thus I stood all the while this attempt was making, with my hair on end and my tongue cleaving to my gullet in a terrible fear, not of the mischief that might befall me, but that in such darkness I might fail to kill him who would harm Lady Biddy.

The latch fell for the second time, and there was no further attempt to open the door, but for a long while I stood there with my knife clenched in my hand.

When I came to reason on this attempt, I concluded that Rodrigues had no hand in it, for it was not his manner to go that way to work, but rather some villain of his crew; whosoever it was, that bolt saved his life for the time, for I do believe that had he been powerful as Hercules, I should have rent him to pieces before he set foot in the chamber where Lady Biddy lay.

I slept no more that night, you may be sure, nor did I deem it safe to put up my knife until the windows in the gallery becoming faintly visible showed that day was at hand. And now, feeling there was no further danger for the present, I opened the little gallery door, and creeping out into the rain, made a shift to cleanse myself somewhat, and set my hair in order, using my fingers for a comb.

By the time this was done, and I had gone back into the cabin, and got my coat, etc., our common safety demanded that I should arouse Lady Biddy, which I did by scratching gently against the partition as we had arranged over-

Q 2

night, and she replied by scratching the wain-
scot on her side. When she was dressed she
came out from her room, and I saw the upper
part of her graceful figure and her small head,
revealed against the light, now pretty well
advanced, on the gallery windows. Then stoop-
ing low that I might not likewise be revealed
to any one peering through the fore windows, I
crept into the cabin she had left, which, to my
senses, was like any flower garden with the
fresh perfume of her breath.

Anon she came back to that chamber, and
giving me her hand, told me (to my question-
ing) that she had slept well; and I told her
nothing of what had happened in the night,
that no trouble should disturb her repose if it
pleased Providence to keep us prisoners there
another night.

Then we fell to discoursing (very low) as to
our conduct during the day. With reluctance
I advised her to keep in the outer chamber,
that Rodrigues might suspect nothing, owning
that for our deliverance I saw no better help

than to be guided by circumstances as they arose.

She made no objection to this counsel. "But," says she, "what shall I do if that villain comes to me?" (meaning Rodrigues).

To this I replied (though it went against the grain), that whilst he behaved civilly she would do well to tolerate his visits and listen to what he said. "For," say I, "though you hold the door, and so exclude him for a minute, he can, if he will, burst it open, and by thus bringing about one act of violence may you lead to another. To force we can only oppose force, and his power is out of all proportion to ours; wherefore it behoves us to use such strategy as we may, for only thus can we live to take advantage of a better opportunity."

"You are right," says she, with such submissiveness in her voice as I had never expected to hear. "I will do as you bid me. But should he overstep the bounds of civility?"

"Then," say I, grinding my teeth, "be sure that, whatever may afterwards befall, he shall die."

Soon after this the boy raps at the outer door, and brings in Lady Biddy's breakfast. Having set it on the table and placed a chair for her very orderly, he moves as if he would go into the inner cabin, when Lady Biddy, catching him quickly by the arm, cries—

"Where are you going, child? What do you want in there?"

"Why, madam," says he, "I am but going to make your bed, and set your cabin in order, as my master bade me."

"Nay," says she, "I can do all there is to be done myself."

With that she leads the boy to the door and sends him away; so was I again saved from discovery.

To make sure that no one was watching her, Lady Biddy pulled up the blinds in the fore windows, and finding she was unobserved, this kind soul, even before she tasted a morsel herself, whips a portion of her victuals into a dish and brings it to me for my comfort, and sure no food was ever so seasoned to excite the appetite as this to which her kindness gave its savour.

As she had brought the dish to me, so she took it away, and at the same time a book from the store of her goods which Rodrigues had caused to be brought into the cabin.

Seating herself on the sofett, she disposed herself to read, yet with little ability to distract her thoughts, for every moment she expected to see Rodrigues; and while she was thus employed, the boy comes to take away the dishes, etc., and this being done and the crumbs swept up, he again crosses towards the inner cabin. Whereupon, in a terrible taking, Lady Biddy, starting up once more, checks him—

"Why will you persevere in entering my chamber," cries she, "when I tell you that I will do all that is necessary there?"

"'Tis no fault of mine," says the child. "My master told me to fetch some clothes of his from the chest, and I must do his bidding."

"Tell me what you need, and I will get it,"

says Lady Biddy, going to the betwixt door; and then seeing at a glance that I had concealed myself, she adds, in a tone of indifference, " Nay, fetch them yourself," and so goes back with her book to the sofett.

I had crept to my old hiding-place under the cot when the boy first came into the next cabin, for fear of accident, and now, as I lay there, I could see all that he did. First of all, he went to the chest and duly laid out a suit of clothes; then taking a quick glance through the half-open door to make sure Lady Biddy was not observing him, he turns about, and going to one corner of the cabin, strips up the carpet, does something to the boards (which I could not see for my position), and then as swiftly turns back the carpet to its place. This done, the little villain shuts-to the drawer of the chest with a bang, and goes out of the room with the clothes in his arms, as if that had been all his errand.

I lost no time in creeping out and crossing to that corner of the cabin to see what the boy

had been about; and, at a glance, I perceived
the whole business as I turned back the carpet.
Here, in the boards, was a hinged hatch or trap-
door with a ring whereby to raise it, and a bolt
to make it secure—ring, bolt, and hinge being
sunk in the boards, flush, and neatly done as
any joiner's work. The bolt was slipped back
so that the trap could be opened from below,
and I doubted not that this had been the work
of that little villain-boy. Moreover, as I had
concluded that he who tried the door in the
night was not Rodrigues, so I surmised that
this undoing of the hatch was not of his order-
ing (since there was no reason for his going
about in this fashion), but rather the indepen-
dent measures of the boy to get into the cabin
for pilfering purposes, or of some one of the
crew who had won over the boy to his will for
more villainous purpose. For the present I
contented myself with shooting back the bolt,
returning the carpet to its place, and getting
back to my hiding-place under the cot.

CHAPTER XXI.

ABOUT noon Rodrigues came into the cabin
where my Lady Biddy sat, with his hair combed,
rings on his fingers, and rigged out in a new
suit of clothes—as fine as any popinjay. Taking
off his hat with a low salute, he observed that
the heavy rain was past, and fairer weather
might be now expected, and so seated himself
with easy insolence near Lady Biddy, who
thereupon rose to her feet, and stood calmly
waiting for him to announce his business
there.

"I have come," says he, "to know if I can
add anything to your convenience or comfort
here during the stay which, as I pointed out
yesterday, circumstances have necessitated."

"You can make my captivity less intolerable," replies Lady Biddy, " by letting me know at once when it is to end."

" If this breeze continues we may fairly expect to be at our journey's end in four days," says he.

" And what do you intend to do with me then ? " asks Lady Biddy.

" Rather let me ask you, madam," says he, with a hideous smile, " what you intend to do with me ? "

" I do not understand what you mean by that," replies Lady Biddy.

" It is for you to command," says he, " and for me to obey in anything that is possible."

" If I demand my freedom—liberty to return to my friends ! " says she, perplexed by his sophistry, for she knew full well that this seeming compliance was but a mask and a snare.

" Certainly," says he, still with that hideous smile, " nothing can be more reasonable ; and if it will give you happiness and promote that better opinion of me, which I hope one day you

will entertain, I shall do my utmost to help you
to find your friends."

Lady Biddy knew not what response to make
to this fine speech, his promises being far too
good to accept for his true intent; so she waited,
looking at him to continue, but with much
disgust and loathing, for there was lust in his
face and devilish wickedness in his eyes, as leaning back on the sofett he surveyed her person
from head to foot, and again brought his gaze
slowly up to her face.

"Pardon me," says he, "your beauty dis-
tracts my thoughts from the subject of our conversation. Where was I? Ah, yes. Santiago
de Léon de Caracas, whither we are now sailing,
is an agreeable place. I have friends there.
You must know that I am a Spanish gentleman
by birth. There is a palace on the side of a
hill facing the sea which I think will prove
to your taste. You who have lived always in
England can have no idea of the beauty of the
country. I am sure you will be enchanted
with it."

"What is this country or its palaces to me?" cries Lady Biddy, beginning to see his drift.

"You must have a roof to shelter you, and I could offer nothing less than a palace."

"I ask but my liberty that I may return to my friends in England."

"As you please," says he, airily. "I think you will change your mind when you see what a lovely place I propose for your home. However, if, after seeing it, you are still minded to return to England, to England you shall return. It will not be far out of that course to run round by the mouth of the Oronoque and take up poor Sir Harry Smidmore, if he be still on the island where the mutineers left him. Nor is there any reason why you should not cruise about in search of your uncle, Sir Bartlemy Pengilly. Thus would your pleasure in going home be unmarred by any anxiety on account of absent friends."

Once more did he pause to gloat on the perplexity and trouble in that dear face, which

I warrant was become deadly pale with dreadful apprehension. His delight in her torture was like nothing but the pleasure of some cat that plays with a poor mouse before tearing it with cruel talons. Nay, I have observed that some men of the baser sort do strangely mingle cruelty with that sort of love they cherish, so that you will see such fellows take pleasure in making women weep.

"For my own part," continues this Rodrigues, with cool audacity, "it is no matter whether I live in the Indies or in Cornwall, so that I be in your company."

Thus did this wicked cynic so reveal his intent that Lady Biddy could no longer doubt what was behind. Yet did she strive to control her indignation, with the faint hope that she misjudged his meaning.

"I do not ask you to go to England," says she. "All I beg is that you set me ashore, and let me make my way home as God shall please to guide me."

"That is impossible, and I should be unworthy of your respect if I consented to such a course. Beauty such as yours is too rare at Santiago to be set light store by. Believe me, you would never be suffered to leave that city if once you set foot in it. You would become the slave and property of the first who could lay his hand on you. I myself should not dare to take you on shore till a priest had given me a legal right to possess you."

"What!" cries she, losing control of her temper; "do you think I will ever consent to become your wife?"

"Yes," he replies, "I think you will when you consider the matter calmly."

And with that he rose, as if to give her opportunity for reflection. But now, her spirit terribly moved with righteous anger, she stopped him.

"Villain," says she, "do you refuse to give me my liberty?"

"If you mean do I refuse to abandon you to such a fate as would be yours in being set alone on shore at Caracas, I reply yes," says he, with less hypocrisy and more plainly than he had yet spoken. " If you refuse to be the wife of a Spanish gentleman you shall certainly not become the slave of a mongrel peasant."

" You intend to keep me an unwilling prisoner on board this ship? "

" I do," says he, " in the hope—nay, in the firm belief—that you will willingly agree to be my wife by the time we reach England."

" In England there are gallows for such rascal pirates as you."

" No," says he, catching hold of her arm ere she could escape his touch, and holding her firmly—" not when they have friends to protect them, and the wit besides to close the mouths of enemies. No one will bring disgrace on Lady Biddy by hanging her husband and the father of her children. For my sake, to save me from the gallows, you will consent to become my wife. If that be not a sufficient reason, then you will marry me for your own sake. The wife of Don Sanchez Rodrigues de Arevalo may hold up her head in the King's court; but the

mistress of Rodrigues, the pirate, flung ashore
at Plymouth, dare not crawl to show her face
in Falmouth. You will see," adds he, freeing
her arm, and with a return to his former hypocritical fair seeming—"you will see that what I
propose is entirely to your advantage, and in-
evitable as the setting of the sun."

Thereupon he makes her another low
obeisance, turns on his heel, and struts out of
the cabin.

All these particulars did Lady Biddy lay
before me when she had bolted the door after
Rodrigues his departure and come into the next
chamber, which she could well do at that time
without arousing suspicion. Many times she
paused and could not speak for indignation and
offended pride; nay, I think she would have
kept this matter to herself, but that I pressed
her to tell all for my better guidance. Tears
she had not one, for passion held them back.

" Does he think," says she, with scorn that
scarce permitted her to bate her voice—" does
he think that ever I will live to be his slave?

R

I could cut this arm off because his foul hand
has touched it.   I will die a thousand deaths
rather than submit to such injury.   Promise
me, Benet, that if you hear me cry for help——"

"Fearn ot," says I, interrupting her.   "My
knife was drawn, and I stood ready by the little
door all the time I heard the muttering of his
voice in there.   So will I stand prepared when
next he comes, and be assured I will have his
life if you cry to me."

"Nay," says she; "take my life first and
his after, for I would not outlive my shame."

I tried to soothe her mind, which was over-
much exalted, and bade her not think of death
while any hope remained, but rather trust to
my ability to effect our escape when we came
to that port he had spoken of.

"And now," says I, "do pray go back, and
seem to make light of this matter; for I fear
that if he be undeceived in his hopes he may
bring the business to an extremity before we get
near land.   Remember, my lady, 'tis not your
own honour alone you have to consider, though

that be paramount to all, but the peace of Sir Bartlemy and," adds I, with an effort, "your poor lover, Sir Harry. Wherefore, for their sakes, must we fight this villain with his own weapons—meeting subtlety with subtlety; and for some little while, if you may subdue your proud spirit, it will be well to let him opine you will in time come round to his way of thinking."

"I understand you, Benet," says she, calmly. "You fear if he thinks my resolution invincible he may"—she paused, covering her face with her hands, and added, leaving a blank where she could not utter her thought—"before we reach Caracas."

"Yes, that is what I do fear," says I.

"I will do my best, Benet," says she, "to follow your guidance, which I see is wise and good. Yet, if I fail—if—if——"

"Nay, I know what you would say; and here," says I, dropping on my knees beside her —"here I swear that at your cry for help I will slay both him and you."

"And with equal sincerity, Benet, I promise you I will not give that signal for my death until it is needed."

There was no need to explain these words more fully. We both understood that her dishonour was alone to call for this sole remedy. And, still on my knees, I vowed that I also would not live to bear the memory of her fate.

.

END OF VOL. I.

PRINTED BY CASSELL & COMPANY, LIMITED, LA BELLE SAUVAGE, LONDON, E.C.

Illustrated, Fine Art, and other Volumes.

Abbeys and Churches of England and Wales, The: Descriptive, Historical, Pictorial. 21s.

After London; or, Wild England. By the late RICHARD JEFFERIES. *Cheap Edition*, 3s. 6d.

Along Alaska's Great River. By Lieut. SCHWATKA. Illustrated. 12s. 6d.

American Penman, An. By JULIAN HAWTHORNE. Boards, 2s.; cloth, 3s. 6d.

American Yachts and Yachting. Illustrated. 6s.

Animal Painting in Water Colours. With Eighteen Coloured Plates by FREDERICK TAYLER. 5s.

Arabian Nights Entertainments (Cassell's). With about 400 Illustrations. 10s. 6d.

Architectural Drawing. By PHENÉ SPIERS. Illustrated. 10s. 6d.

Art, The Magazine of. Yearly Volume. With several hundred Engravings, and Twelve Etchings, Photogravures, &c. 16s.

Behind Time. By G. P. LATHROP. Illustrated. 2s. 6d.

Bimetallism, The Theory of. By D. BARBOUR. 6s.

Bismarck, Prince. By C. LOWE, M.A. Two Vols. *Cheap Edition.* 10s. 6d.

Black Arrow, The. A Tale of the Two Roses. By R. L. STEVENSON. 5s.

British Ballads. 275 Original Illustrations. Two Vols. Cloth, 7s. 6d. each.

British Battles on Land and Sea. By the late JAMES GRANT. With about 600 Illustrations. Three Vols., 4to, £1 7s.; Library Edition, £1 10s.

British Battles, Recent. Illustrated. 4to, 9s. Library Edition, 10s.

British Empire, The. By SIR GEORGE CAMPBELL. 3s.

Browning, An Introduction to the Study of. By ARTHUR SYMONS. 2s. 6d.

Butterflies and Moths, European. By W. F. KIRBY. With 61 Coloured Plates. Demy 4to, 35s.

Canaries and Cage-Birds, The Illustrated Book of. By W. A. BLAKSTON, W. SWAYSLAND, and A. F. WIENER. With 56 Fac-simile Coloured Plates, 35s.

Cannibals and Convicts. By JULIAN THOMAS ("The Vagabond"). *Cheap Edition*, 5s.

Captain Trafalgar. By WESTALL and LAURIE. Illustrated. 5s.

Cassell's Family Magazine. Yearly Vol. Illustrated. 9s.

Celebrities of the Century: Being a Dictionary of Men and Women of the Nineteenth Century. 21s.; roxburgh, 25s.

Changing Year, The. With Illustrations. 7s. 6d.

Chess Problem, The. With Illustrations by C. PLANCK and others. 7s. 6d.

Children of the Cold, The. By Lieut. SCHWATKA. 2s. 6d.

China Painting. By FLORENCE LEWIS. With Sixteen Coloured Plates, and a selection of Wood Engravings. With full Instructions. 5s.

Choice Dishes at Small Cost. By A. G. PAYNE. *Cheap Edition*, 1s.

Christmas in the Olden Time. By Sir WALTER SCOTT. With charming Original Illustrations. 7s. 6d.

Cities of the World. Three Vols. Illustrated. 7s. 6d. each.

Civil Service, Guide to Employment in the. *New and Enlarged Edition.* 3s. 6d.

Civil Service.—Guide to Female Employment in Government Offices. Cloth, 1s.

Clinical Manuals for Practitioners and Students of Medicine. (*A List of Volumes forwarded post free on application to the Publishers.*)

Clothing, The Influence of, on Health. By FREDERICK TREVES, F.R.C.S. 2s.

Cobden Club, Some Works published for the:—

Writings of Richard Cobden. 6s.	Our Land Laws of the Past. 3d.
Local Government and Taxation in the United Kingdom. 5s.	The Caribbean Confederation. By C. S. Salmon. 1s. 6d
Displacement of Labour and Capital. 3d.	Pleas for Protection Examined. By A. Mon-
Free Trade versus Fair Trade. 5s.	gredien. *New and Revised Edition.* 6d.
Free Trade and English Commerce. By A. Mongredien. 6d.	What Protection does for the Farmer. By J. S. Leadam, M.A. 6d.
Crown Colonies. 1s.	The Old Poor Law and the New Socialism;
Popular Fallacies Regarding Trade. 6d.	or, Pauperism and Taxation. By F. C.
Western Farmer of America. 3d.	Montague. 6d.
Reform of the English Land System. 3d.	The Secretary of State for India in Coun-
Fair Trade Unmasked. By G. W. Medley. 6d.	oil. 6d.
Technical Education. By F. C. Mon-	The National Income and Taxation. By
tague, M.A. 6d.	Sir Louis Mallet. 6d.

Colonies and India, Our: How we Got Them, and Why we Keep Them. By Prof. C. RANSOME. 1s.
Colour. By Prof. A. H. CHURCH. *New and Enlarged Edition*, with Coloured Plates. 3s. 6d.
Columbus, Christopher, The Life and Voyages of. By WASHINGTON IRVING. Three Vols. 7s. 6d.
Commodore Junk. By G. MANVILLE FENN. 5s.
Cookery, Cassell's Shilling. The Largest and Best Work on the Subject ever produced. 1s.
Cookery, Cassell's Dictionary of. Containing about Nine Thousand Recipes. 7s. 6d. ; roxburgh, 10s. 6d.
Cookery, A Year's. By PHYLLIS BROWNE. Cloth gilt or oiled cloth, 3s. 6d.
Cook Book, Catherine Owen's New. 4s.
Co-operators, Working Men: What They have Done, and What They are Doing. By A. H. DYKE-ACLAND, M.P., and B. JONES. 1s.
Countries of the World, The. By ROBERT BROWN, M.A., Ph.D., &c. Complete in Six Vols., with about 750 Illustrations. 4to, 7s. 6d. each.
Culmshire Folk. By the Author of "John Orlebar," &c. 3s. 6d.
Cyclopædia, Cassell's Concise. With 12,000 subjects, brought down to the latest date. With about 600 Illustrations, 15s. ; roxburgh, 18s.
Cyclopædia, Cassell's Miniature. Containing 30,000 Subjects. Cloth, 3s. 6d.
Dairy Farming. By Prof. J. P. SHELDON. With 25 Fac-simile Coloured Plates, and numerous Wood Engravings. Demy 4to, 21s.
Dead Man's Rock. A Romance. By Q. 5s.
Decisive Events in History. By THOMAS ARCHER. With Sixteen Illustrations. Boards, 3s. 6d. ; cloth, 5s.
Deserted Village Series, The. Consisting of *Éditions de luxe* of favourite poems · by Standard Authors. Illustrated. Cloth gilt, 2s. 6d.

Goldsmith's Deserted Village.	Wordsworth's Ode on Immortality,
Milton's L'Allegro and Il Ponsoroso.	and Lines on Tintern Abbey.
Songs from Shakespeare.	

Dickens, Character Sketches from. FIRST, SECOND, and THIRD SERIES. With Six Original Drawings in each, by FREDERICK BARNARD. In Portfolio, 21s. each.
Diary of Two Parliaments. By H. W. LUCY. The Disraeli Parliament, 12s. The Gladstone Parliament, 12s.
Dog, The. By IDSTONE. Illustrated. 2s. 6d.
Dog, Illustrated Book of the. By VERO SHAW, B.A. With 28 Coloured Plates. Cloth bevelled, 35s. ; half-morocco, 45s.
Dog Stories and Dog Lore. By Col. THOS. W. KNOX. 6s.
Domestic Dictionary, The. An Encyclopædia for the Household. Cloth, 7s. 6d.
Doré's Dante's Inferno. Illustrated by GUSTAVE DORÉ. *Popular Edition*, 21s.
Doré's Dante's Purgatorio and Paradiso. Illustrated by GUSTAVE DORÉ. *Popular Edition*. 21s.
Doré's Fairy Tales Told Again. With 24 Full-page Engravings by DORÉ. 5s.
Doré Gallery, The. With 250 Illustrations by GUSTAVE DORÉ. 4to, 42s.
Doré's Milton's Paradise Lost. With Full-page Drawings by GUSTAVE DORÉ. 4to, 21s.
Earth, Our, and Its Story. By Dr. ROBERT BROWN, F.L.S. Vol. I., with Coloured Plates and numerous Wood Engravings. 9s.
Edinburgh, Old and New, Cassell's. With 600 Illustrations. Three Vols., 9s. each ; library binding, £1 10s. the set.
Egypt: Descriptive, Historical, and Picturesque. By Prof. G. EBERS. Translated by CLARA BELL, with Notes by SAMUEL BIRCH, LL.D., &c. *Popular Edition*, in Two Vols., 42s.
"89." A Novel. By EDGAR HENRY. Cloth, 3s. 6d.
Electricity, Age of, from Amber Soul to Telephone. By PARK BENJAMIN, Ph.D. 7s. 6d.
Electricity, Practical. By Prof. W. E. AYRTON. Illustrated. 7s. 6d.
Electricity in the Service of Man. With nearly 850 Illustrations. 21s.
Encyclopædic Dictionary, The. A New and Original Work of Reference to all the Words in the English Language. Complete in Fourteen Divisional Vols., 10s. 6d. each ; or Seven Vols., half-morocco, 21s. each.
England, Cassell's Illustrated History of. With 2,000 Illustrations. Ten Vols., 4to, 9s. each. *New and Revised Edition.* Vols. I. and II., 9s. each.

English History, The Dictionary of. Cloth, 21s. ; roxburgh, 25s.
English Literature, Library of. By Prof. HENRY MORLEY. Complete in 5 vols., 7s. 6d. each.

VOL. I.—SHORTER ENGLISH POEMS.	VOL. IV.—SHORTER WORKS IN ENGLISH
VOL II.—ILLUSTRATIONS OF ENGLISH	PROSE.
RELIGION.	VOL. V.—SKETCHES OF LONGER WORKS IN
VOL. III.—ENGLISH PLAYS.	ENGLISH VERSE AND PROSE.

English Literature, Morley's First Sketch of. *Revised Edition,* 7s. 6d.
English Literature, The Dictionary of. By W. DAVENPORT ADAMS. *Cheap Edition,* 7s. 6d. ; roxburgh, 10s. 6d.
English Literature, The Story of. By ANNA BUCKLAND. *New and Cheap Edition.* 3s. 6d.
English Writers. An attempt towards a History of English Literature. By HENRY MORLEY, LL.D., Professor of English Literature, University College, London. Vols. I., II., III., and IV., 5s. each.
Æsop's Fables. With about 150 Illustrations by E. GRISET. *Cheap Edition,* cloth, 3s. 6d. ; bevelled boards, gilt edges, 5s.
Etching: Its Technical Processes, with Remarks on Collections and Collecting. By S. K. KOEHLER. Illustrated with 30 Full-page Plates. Price £4 4s.
Etiquette of Good Society. 1s. ; cloth, 1s. 6d.
Eye, Ear, and Throat, The Management of the. 3s. 6d.
Family Physician, The. By Eminent PHYSICIANS and SURGEONS. *New and Revised Edition.* Cloth, 21s. ; roxburgh, 25s.
Fenn, G. Manville, Works by. *Popular Editions.* Boards, 2s. each ; or cloth, 2s. 6d.

Dutch the Diver; or, a Man's Mistake.	Poverty Corner.
My Patients.	The Vicar's People. } In Cloth only.
The Parson o' Dumford.	Sweet Mace. }

Ferns, European. By JAMES BRITTEN, F.L.S. With 30 Fac-simile Coloured Plates by D. BLAIR, F.L.S. 21s.
Field Naturalist's Handbook, The. By Rev. J. G. WOOD & THEODORE WOOD. 5s.
Figuier's Popular Scientific Works. With Several Hundred Illustrations in each. 3s. 6d. each.

The Human Race.	The Ocean World.
World Before the Deluge.	The Vegetable World.
Reptiles and Birds.	The Insect World.
Mammalia.	

Figure Painting in Water Colours. With 16 Coloured Plates by BLANCHE MACARTHUR and JENNIE MOORE. With full Instructions. 7s. 6d.
Fine-Art Library, The. Edited by JOHN SPARKES, Principal of the South Kensington Art Schools. Each Book contains about 100 Illustrations. 5s. each.

Tapestry. By Eugène Müntz. Translated by Miss L. J. Davis.	The Education of the Artist. By Ernest Chesneau. Translated by Clara Bell. Now illustrated.
Engraving. By Le Vicomte Henri Delaborde. Translated by R. A. M. Stevenson.	Greek Archæology. By Maxime Collignon. Translated by Dr. J. H. Wright.
The English School of Painting. By E. Chesneau. Translated by L. N. Etherington. With an Introduction by Prof. Ruskin.	Artistic Anatomy. By Prof. Duval. Translated by F. E. Fenton.
The Flemish School of Painting. By A. J. Wauters. Translated by Mrs. Henry Rossel.	The Dutch School of Painting. By Henry Havard. Translated by G. Powell.

Five Pound Note, The, and other Stories. By G. S. JEALOUS. 1s.
Flower Painting in Water Colours. First and Second Series. With 20 Fac-simile Coloured Plates in each by F. E. HULME, F.L.S., F.S.A. With Instructions by the Artist. Interleaved. 5s. each.
Flower Painting, Elementary. With Eight Coloured Plates. 3s.
Flowers, and How to Paint Them. By MAUD NAFTEL. With Coloured Plates. 5s.
Forging of the Anchor, The. A Poem. By the late Sir SAMUEL FERGUSON, LL.D. With 20 Original Illustrations. Gilt edges, 5s.
Fossil Reptiles, A History of British. By Sir RICHARD OWEN, K.C.B., F.R.S., &c. With 268 Plates. In Four Vols., £12 12s.
France as It Is. By ANDRÉ LEBON and PAUL PELET. With Three Maps. Crown 8vo, cloth, 7s. 6d.
Franco-German War, Cassell's History of the. Two Vols. With 500 Illustrations. 9s. each.
Fresh-Water Fishes of Europe, The. By Prof. H. G. SEELEY, F.R.S. *Cheap Edition.* 7s. 6d.
Garden Flowers, Familiar. By SHIRLEY HIBBERD. With Coloured Plates by F. E. HULME, F.L.S. Complete in Five Series. Cloth gilt, 12s. 6d. each.
Gardening, Cassell's Popular. Illustrated. Complete in 4 Vols., 5s. each.
Geometrical Drawing for Army Candidates. By H. T. LILLEY, M.A. 2s.

Geometry, First Elements of Experimental. By PAUL BERT. 1s. 6d.
Geometry, Practical Solid. By Major ROSS. 2s.
Germany, William of. By ARCHIBALD FORBES. 3s. 6d.
Gladstone, Life of the Rt. Hon. W. E. By G. BARNETT SMITH. With Portrait. 3s. 6d.
Gleanings from Popular Authors. Two Vols. With Original Illustrations. 4to, 9s. each. Two Vols. in One, 15s.
Gold to Grey, From. Being Poems and Pictures of Life and Nature. By MARY D. BRINE. Illustrated. 7s. 6d.
Great Bank Robbery, The. A Novel. By JULIAN HAWTHORNE. Boards, 2s.
Great Industries of Great Britain. With 400 Illustrations. 3 Vols., 7s. 6d. each.
Great Northern Railway, The Official Illustrated Guide to the. 1s.; cloth, 2s.
Great Western Railway, The Official Illustrated Guide to the. 1s.; cloth, 2s.
Great Painters of Christendom, The, from Cimabue to Wilkie. By JOHN FORBES-ROBERTSON. Illustrated throughout. *Popular Edition,* cloth gilt, 12s. 6d.
Gulliver's Travels. With 88 Engravings by MORTEN. *Cheap Edition.* Cloth, 3s. 6d.; cloth gilt, 5s.
Gum Boughs and Wattle Bloom. By DONALD MACDONALD. 5s.
Gun and its Development, The. By W. W. GREENER. Illustrated. 10s. 6d.
Guns, Modern Shot. By W. W. GREENER. Illustrated. 5s.
Health at School. By CLEMENT DUKES, M.D., B.S. 7s. 6d. [burgh, 25s.
Health, The Book of. By Eminent Physicians and Surgeons. Cloth, 21s.; rox-
Health, The Influence of Clothing on. By F. TREVES, F.R.C.S. 2s.
Heavens, The Story of the. By Sir ROBERT STAWELL BALL, LL.D., F.R.S., Royal Astronomer of Ireland. Coloured Plates and Wood Engravings. 31s. 6d.
Heroes of Britain in Peace and War. In Two Vols., with 300 Original Illustrations. 5s. each; or One Vol., library binding, 10s. 6d.
Holy Land and the Bible, The. By the Rev. CUNNINGHAM GEIKIE, D.D. With Map. Two Vols. 24s.
Homes, Our, and How to Make them Healthy. By Eminent Authorities. Illustrated. 15s.; roxburgh, 18s.
Horse-Keeper, The Practical. By GEORGE FLEMING, LL.D., F.R.C.V.S. Illustrated. Crown 8vo, cloth, 7s. 6d.
Horse, The Book of the. By SAMUEL SIDNEY. With 28 *fac-simile* Coloured Plates. Demy 4to, 35s.; half-morocco, £2 5s.
Horses, The Simple Ailments of. By W. F. Illustrated. 5s.
Household Guide, Cassell's. With Illustrations and Coloured Plates. *New and Revised Edition,* complete in Four Vols., 20s.
How Dante Climbed the Mountain. By ROSE EMILY SELFE. With Eight Full-page Engravings by GUSTAVE DORÉ. 2s.
How Women may Earn a Living. By MERCY GROGAN. 1s.
Imperial White Books. In Quarterly Vols. 10s. 6d. per annum, post free; to subscribers separately, 3s. 6d. each.
India, Cassell's History of. By the late JAMES GRANT. With 400 Illustrations. 15s.
India : the Land and the People. By Sir JAMES CAIRD, K.C.B. 10s. 6d.
In-door Amusements, Card Games, and Fireside Fun, Cassell's. 3s. 6d.
Industrial Remuneration Conference. The Report of. 2s. 6d.
Insect Variety: its Propagation and Distribution. By A. H. SWINTON. 7s. 6d.
Irish Parliament, The, What it Was, and What it Did. By J. G. SWIFT McNEILL, M.A., M.P. 1s.
Irish Parliament, A Miniature History of the. By J. C. HASLAM. 3d.
Irish Union ; Before and After. By A. K. CONNELL, M.A. 2s. 6d.
John Parmelee's Curse. By JULIAN HAWTHORNE. 2s. 6d.
Kennel Guide, Practical. By Dr. GORDON STABLES. Illustrated. *Cheap Edition.* 1s.
Kidnapped. By R. L. STEVENSON. *Illustrated Edition.* 5s.
King Solomon's Mines. By H. RIDER HAGGARD. *Illustrated Edition.* 5s.
Khiva, A Ride to. By Col. FRED BURNABY. 1s. 6d.
Ladies' Physician, The. By a London Physician. 6s.
Lady Biddy Fane. By FRANK BARRETT. Three Vols. Cloth, 31s. 6d.
Lady's World, The. An Illustrated Magazine of Fashion and Society. Yrly. Vol. 18s.
Land Question, The. By Prof. J. ELLIOT, M.R.A.C. Including the Land Scare and Production of Cereals. 3s. 6d.
Landscape Painting in Oils, A Course of Lessons in. By A. F. GRACE, With Nine Reproductions in Colour. *Cheap Edition.* 25s.

Law, About Going to. By A. J. WILLIAMS, M.P. 2s. 6d.

Laws of Every Day Life, The. By H. O. ARNOLD-FORSTER. 1s. 6d.

Letts's Diaries and other Time-saving Publications are now published exclusively by CASSELL & COMPANY. (*A List sent post free on application.*)

Local Dual Standards. By JOHN HENRY NORMAN. Gold and Silver Standard Currencies. 1s.

Local Government in England and Germany. By the Rt. Hon. Sir ROBERT MORIER, G.C.B., &c. 1s.

London, Brighton, and South Coast Railway, The Official Illustrated Guide to the. 1s.; cloth, 2s.

London and North Western Railway, The Official Illustrated Guide to the. 1s.; cloth, 2s.

London and South Western Railway, The Official Illustrated Guide to the. 1s.; cloth, 2s.

London, Greater. By EDWARD WALFORD. Two Vols. With about 400 Illustrations. 9s. each. *Library Edition.* Two Vols. £1 the set.

London, Old and New. By WALTER THORNBURY and EDWARD WALFORD. Six Vols., each containing about 200 Illustrations and Maps. Cloth, 9s. each. *Library Edition.* Imitation roxburgh. £3.

Longfellow, H. W., Choice Poems by. Illustrated by his Son, ERNEST W. LONGFELLOW. 6s.

Longfellow's Poetical Works. *Fine-Art Edition.* Illustrated throughout with Original Engravings. Royal 4to, cloth gilt, £3 3s. *Popular Edition.* 16s.

Luther, Martin: the Man and his Work. By PETER BAYNE, LL.D. Two Vols., 24s.

Marine Painting. By WALTER W. MAY, R.I. With 16 Coloured Plates. Cloth, 5s.

Mechanics, The Practical Dictionary of. Containing 15,000 Drawings. Four Vols. 21s. each.

Medicine, Manuals for Students of. (*A List forwarded post free on application.*)

Midland Railway, The Official Illustrated Guide to the. *New and Revised Edition.* 1s.; cloth, 2s.

Modern Europe, A History of. By C. A. FYFFE, M.A. Vol. I. From 1792 to 1814. 12s. Vol. II. From 1814 to 1848. 12s.

Music, Illustrated History of. By EMIL NAUMANN. Edited by the Rev. Sir F. A. GORE OUSELEY, Bart. Illustrated. Two Vols. 31s. 6d.

National Library, Cassell's. In Weekly Volumes, each containing about 192 pages. Paper covers, 3d.; cloth, 6d. (*A List of the Volumes already published sent post free on application.*)

Natural History, Cassell's Concise. By E. PERCEVAL WRIGHT, M.A., M.D., F.L.S. With several Hundred Illustrations. 7s. 6d.; roxburgh, 10s. 6d.

Natural History, Cassell's New. Edited by Prof. P. MARTIN DUNCAN, M.B., F.R.S., F.G.S. With Contributions by Eminent Scientific Writers. Complete in Six Vols. With about 2,000 high-class Illustrations. Extra crown 4to, cloth, 9s. each.

Nature, Short Studies from. Illustrated. *Cheap Edition.* 2s. 6d.

Neutral Tint, A Course of Painting in. With Twenty-four Plates by R. P. LEITCH. With full Instructions to the Pupil. 5s.

Nimrod in the North; or, Hunting and Fishing Adventures in the Arctic Regions. By Lieut. SCHWATKA. Illustrated. 7s. 6d.

Nursing for the Home and for the Hospital, A Handbook of. By CATHERINE J. WOOD. *Cheap Edition.* 1s. 6d.; cloth, 2s.

Oil Painting, A Manual of. By Hon. JOHN COLLIER. Cloth, 2s. 6d.

On the Equator. By H. DE W. Illustrated with Photos. 3s. 6d.

Orion the Gold Beater. A Novel. By SYLVANUS COBB, Junr. Cloth, 3s. 6d.

Our Own Country. Six Vols. With 1,200 Illustrations. Cloth, 7s. 6d. each.

Outdoor Sports and Indoor Amusements, Cassell's Book of. With about 900 Illustrations. *Cheap Edition.* 992 pages, medium 8vo, cloth, 3s. 6d.

Paris, Cassell's Illustrated Guide to. Cloth, 2s.

Parliaments, A Diary of Two. By H. W. LUCY. The Disraeli Parliament, 1874—1880. 12s. The Gladstone Parliament, 1881—1886. 12s.

Paxton's Flower Garden. By Sir JOSEPH PAXTON and Prof. LINDLEY. Revised by THOMAS BAINES, F.R.H.S. Three Vols. With 100 Coloured Plates. £1 1s. each.

Peoples of the World, The. By Dr. ROBERT BROWN. Complete in Six Volumes. With Illustrations. 7s. 6d. each.

Phantom City, The. By W. WESTALL. 5s.

Photography for Amateurs. By T. C. HEPWORTH. Illustrated, 1s.; or cloth, 1s. 6d.

Phrase and Fable, Dictionary of. By the Rev. Dr. BREWER. *Cheap Edition,* Enlarged, cloth, 3s. 6d. ; or with leather back, 4s. 6d.

Picturesque America. Complete in Four Vols., with 48 Exquisite Steel Plates, and about 800 Original Wood Engravings. £2 2s. each.

Picturesque Canada. With about 600 Original Illustrations. Two Vols., £3 3s. each.

Picturesque Europe. Complete in Five Vols. Each containing 13 Exquisite Steel Plates, from Original Drawings, and nearly 200 Original Illustrations. £10 10s. ; half-morocco, £15 15s. ; morocco gilt, £26 5s. The POPULAR EDITION is now complete in Five Vols., 18s. each.

Pigeon Keeper, The Practical. By LEWIS WRIGHT. Illustrated. 3s. 6d.

Pigeons, The Book of. By ROBERT FULTON. Edited by LEWIS WRIGHT. With 50 Coloured Plates and numerous Wood Engravings. 31s. 6d. ; half-morocco, £2 2s.

Pocket Guide to Europe (Cassell's). Size 5½ in. × 3¾ in. Leather, 6s.

Poems, Representative of Living Poets, American and English. Selected by the Poets themselves. 15s.

Poets, Cassell's Miniature Library of the :—

Burns. Two Vols. Cloth, 1s. each ; or cloth, gilt edges, 2s. 6d. the set.
Byron. Two Vols. Cloth, 1s. each ; or cloth, gilt edges, 2s. 6d. the set.
Hood. Two Vols. Cloth, 1s. each ; or cloth, gilt edges, 2s. 6d. the set.
Longfellow. Two Vols. Cloth, 1s. each ; or cloth, gilt edges, 2s. 6d. the set.
Milton. Two Vols. Cloth, 1s. each ; or cloth, gilt edges, 2s. 6d. the set.
Scott. Two Vols. Cloth, 1s. each ; or cloth, gilt edges, 2s. 6d. the set.
Sheridan and Goldsmith. 2 Vols. Cloth, 1s. each ; or cloth, gilt edges, 2s. 6d. the set.
Wordsworth. Two Vols. Cloth, 1s. each ; or cloth, gilt edges, 2s. 6d. the set.
Shakespeare. Twelve Vols., half cloth, in box, 12s.

Popular Library, Cassell's. A Series of New and Original Works. Cloth, 1s. each.

The Russian Empire.
The Religious Revolution in the Sixteenth Century.
English Journalism.
Our Colonial Empire.
The Young Man in the Battle of Life.
John Wesley.
The Story of the English Jacobins.
Domestic Folk Lore.
The Rev. Rowland Hill.
Boswell and Johnson.
History of the Free-Trade Movement in England.

Post Office of Fifty Years Ago, The. 1s.

Poultry Keeper, The Practical. By LEWIS WRIGHT. With Coloured Plates and Illustrations. 3s. 6d.

Poultry, The Book of. By LEWIS WRIGHT. *Popular Edition.* With Illustrations on Wood. 10s. 6d.

Poultry, The Illustrated Book of. By LEWIS WRIGHT. With Fifty Exquisite Coloured Plates, and numerous Wood Engravings. Cloth, 31s. 6d. ; half-morocco, £2 2s.

Pre-Raphælites (The Italian) in the National Gallery. By COSMO MONKHOUSE. Illustrated. 1s.

Printing Machinery and Letterpress Printing, Modern. By FRED. J. F. WILSON and DOUGLAS GREY. Illustrated. 21s.

Queen Victoria, The Life and Times of. By ROBERT WILSON. Complete in 2 Vols. With numerous Illustrations, representing the Chief Events in the Life of the Queen, and Portraits of the Leading Celebrities of her Reign. Extra crown 4to, cloth gilt, 9s. each.

Queer Race, A. By W. WESTALL. 5s.

Rabbit-Keeper, The Practical. By CUNICULUS. Illustrated. 3s. 6d.

Red Library of English and American Classics, The. Stiff covers, 1s. each ; cloth, 2s. each.

People I have Met.
The Pathfinder.
Evelina.
Scott's Poems.
Last of the Barons.
Adventures of Mr. Ledbury and his friend Jack Johnson.
Ivanhoe.
Oliver Twist.
Selections from Hood's Works.
Longfellow's Prose Works.
Sense and Sensibility.
Lytton's Plays.
Tales, Poems, and Sketches (Bret Harte).
Martin Chuzzlewit. Two Vols.
The Prince of the House of David.
Sheridan's Plays.
Uncle Tom's Cabin.
Deerslayer.
Eugene Aram.
Jack Hinton, the Guardsman.
The Talisman.
Rome and the Early Christians.
The Trials of Margaret Lyndsay.
Edgar Allan Poe. Prose and Poetry, Selections from.
Old Mortality.
The Hour and the Man.
Washington Irving's Sketch-Book.
Last Days of Palmyra.
Tales of the Borders.
Pride and Prejudice.
Last of the Mohicans.
Heart of Midlothian.
Last Days of Pompeii.
Yellowplush Papers.
Handy Andy.
Selected Plays.
American Humour.
Sketches by Boz.
Macaulay's Lays and Selected Essays.
Harry Lorrequer.
Old Curiosity Shop.
Rienzi.
Pickwick (Two Vols.).
Scarlet Letter.

Royal River, The: The Thames, from Source to Sea. With Descriptive Text and a Series of beautiful Engravings. £2 2s.

Russia. By Sir DONALD MACKENZIE WALLACE, M.A. 5s.

Russo-Turkish War, Cassell's History of. With about 500 Illustrations. Two Vols., 9s. each ; library binding, One Vol., 15s.

Saturday Journal, Cassell's. Yearly Vols., 7s. 6d.

Science for All. Edited by Dr. ROBERT BROWN, M.A., F.L.S., &c. With 1,500 Illustrations. Five Vols., 9s. each.

Sea, The: Its Stirring Story of Adventure, Peril, and Heroism. By F. WHYMPER. With 400 Illustrations. Four Vols., 7s. 6d. each.

Section 558, or the Fatal Letter. A Novel. By JULIAN HAWTHORNE. Boards, 2s. ; cloth, 2s. 6d.

Sent Back by the Angels. And other Ballads of Home and Homely Life. By FREDERICK LANGBRIDGE, M.A. 4s. 6d. *Popular Edition,* 1s.

Sepia Painting, A Course of. Two Vols., with Twelve Coloured Plates in each, and numerous Engravings. Each, 3s. Also in One Volume, 5s.

Shaftesbury, The Seventh Earl of, K.G., The Life and Work of. By EDWIN HODDER. With Portraits. Three Vols., 36s. *Popular Edition,* in One Vol., 7s. 6d.

Shakspere, The International. *Édition de luxe.*
"King Henry IV." Illustrated by Herr EDUARD GRÜTZNER. £3 10s.
"As You Like It." Illustrated by Mons. EMILE BAYARD. £3 10s.
"Romeo and Juliet." Illustrated by FRANK DICKSEE, A.R.A. £5 5s.

Shakspere, The Leopold. With 400 Illustrations, and an Introduction by F. J. FURNIVALL. Small 4to, cloth gilt, 7s. 6d. ; half-morocco, 10s. 6d. ; full morocco, £1 1s. *Cheap Edition.* 3s. 6d.

Shakspere, The Royal. With Exquisite Steel Plates and Wood Engravings. Three Vols. 15s. each.

Shakespeare, Cassell's Quarto Edition. Edited by CHARLES and MARY COWDEN CLARKE, and containing about 600 Illustrations by H. C. SELOUS. Complete in Three Vols., cloth gilt, £3 3s.—Also published in Three separate Volumes, in cloth, viz :—The COMEDIES, 21s. ; The HISTORICAL PLAYS, 18s. 6d. ; The TRAGEDIES, 25s.

Shakespeare, Miniature. Illustrated. In Twelve Vols., in box, 12s. ; or in Red Paste Grain (box to match), with spring catch, lettered in gold, 21s.

Shakespearean Scenes and Characters. Illustrative of Thirty Plays of Shakespeare. With Thirty Steel Plates and Ten Wood Engravings. The Text written by AUSTIN BRERETON. Royal 4to, 21s.

Sketching from Nature in Water Colours. By AARON PENLEY. With Illustrations in Chromo-Lithography. 15s.

Skin and Hair, The Management of the. By MALCOLM MORRIS, F.R.C.S. 2s.

Sonnets and Quatorzains. By CHRYS, M.A. (Oxon). 5s.

Standards, Local Dual. By JOHN HENRY NORMAN. 1s.

Steam Engine, The Theory and Action of the: for Practical Men. By W. H. NORTHCOTT, C.E. 3s. 6d.

Stock Exchange Year-Book, The. By THOMAS SKINNER. 12s. 6d.

Summer Tide, Little Folks Holiday Number. 1s.

Sunlight and Shade. With numerous Exquisite Engravings. 7s. 6d.

Surgery, Memorials of the Craft of, in England. With an Introduction by Sir JAMES PAGET. 21s.

Thackeray, Character Sketches from. Six New and Original Drawings by FREDERICK BARNARD, reproduced in Photogravure. 21s.

Thorah, The Yoke of the. A Novel. By SIDNEY LUSKA. Boards, 2s. ; cloth, 3s. 6d.

Three and Sixpenny Library of Standard Tales, &c. All Illustrated and bound in cloth gilt. Crown 8vo. 3s. 6d. each.

Jane Austen and her Works.	Peggy Oglivie's Inheritance.
Mission Life in Greece and Palestine.	The Family Honour.
The Romance of Trade.	Esther West.
The Three Homes.	Working to Win.
Deepdale Vicarage.	Krilof and his Fables. By W. R. S.
In Duty Bound.	Ralston, M.A.
The Half Sisters.	Fairy Tales. By Prof. Morley.

Tot Book for all Public Examinations. By W. S. THOMSON, M.A. 1s.

Town Holdings. 1s.

Tragedy of Brinkwater, The. A Novel. By MARTHA L. MOODEY. Boards, 2s.; cloth, 3s. 6d.
Tragic Mystery, A. A Novel. By JULIAN HAWTHORNE. Boards, 2s. ; cloth, 3s. 6d.
Treasure Island. By R. L. STEVENSON. Illustrated. 5s.
Tree Painting in Water Colours. By W. H. J. BOOT. With Eighteen Coloured Plates, and valuable instructions by the Artist. 5s.
Trees, Familiar. By G. S. BOULGER, F.L.S., F.G.S. Two Series. With Forty full-page Coloured Plates, from Original Paintings by W. H. J. BOOT. 12s. 6d. each.
Twenty Photogravures of Pictures in the Salon of 1885, by the leading French Artists. In Portfolio. Only a limited number of copies have been produced, terms for which can be obtained of all Booksellers.
"Unicode": The Universal Telegraphic Phrase Book. Pocket and Desk Editions. 2s 6d. each.
United States, Cassell's History of the. By the late EDMUND OLLIER. With 600 Illustrations. Three Vols. 9s. each.
United States, The Youth's History of. By EDWARD S. ELLIS. Illustrated. Four Vols. 36s.
Universal History, Cassell's Illustrated. With nearly ONE THOUSAND ILLUSTRATIONS. Vol. I. Early and Greek History.—Vol. II. The Roman Period.—Vol. III. The Middle Ages.—Vol. IV. Modern History. 9s. each.
Vaccination Vindicated. An Answer to the leading Anti-Vaccinators. By JOHN C. McVAIL, M.D., D.P.H. Camb. 5s.
Veiled Beyond, The. A Novel. By S. B. ALEXANDER. Cloth, 3s. 6d.
Vicar of Wakefield and other Works by OLIVER GOLDSMITH. Illustrated. 3s. 6d. ; cloth, gilt edges, 5s.
Water-Colour Painting, A Course of. With Twenty-four Coloured Plates by R. P. LEITCH, and full Instructions to the Pupil. 5s.
What Girls Can Do. By PHYLLIS BROWNE. 2s. 6d.
Who is John Noman? A Novel. By CHARLES HENRY BECKETT. Boards, 2s.; Cloth, 3s. 6d.
Wild Birds, Familiar. By W. SWAYSLAND. Four Series. With 40 Coloured Plates in each. 12s. 6d. each.
Wild Flowers, Familiar. By F. E. HULME, F.L.S., F.S.A. Five Series. With 40 Coloured Plates in each. 12s. 6d. each.
Wise Woman, The. By GEORGE MACDONALD. 2s. 6d.
Woman's World, The. Yearly Volume. 18s.
World of Wit and Humour, The. With 400 Illustrations. Cloth, 7s. 6d. ; cloth gilt, gilt edges, 10s. 6d.
World of Wonders, The. Two Vols. With 400 Illustrations. 7s. 6d. each.
World's Lumber Room, The. By SELINA GAYE. Illustrated. 2s. 6d.
Yule Tide. CASSELL'S CHRISTMAS ANNUAL. 1s.

ILLUSTRATED MAGAZINES.

The Quiver, for Sunday and General Reading. Monthly, 6d.
Cassell's Family Magazine. Monthly, 7d.
"Little Folks" Magazine. Monthly, 6d.
The Magazine of Art. Monthly, 1s.
The Woman's World. Monthly, 1s.
Cassell's Saturday Journal. Weekly, 1d. ; Monthly, 6d.

⁂ Full particulars of CASSELL & COMPANY'S **Monthly Serial Publications** *will be found in* CASSELL & COMPANY'S COMPLETE CATALOGUE.

Catalogues of CASSELL & COMPANY'S PUBLICATIONS, which may be had at all Booksellers', or will be sent post free on application to the Publishers :—
CASSELL'S COMPLETE CATALOGUE, containing particulars of One Thousand Volumes.
CASSELL'S CLASSIFIED CATALOGUE, in which their Works are arranged according to price, from *Threepence to Twenty-five Guineas.*
CASSELL'S EDUCATIONAL CATALOGUE, containing particulars of CASSELL & COMPANY'S Educational Works and Students' Manuals.

CASSELL & COMPANY, LIMITED, *Ludgate Hill, London.*

Bibles and Religious Works.

Bible, The Crown Illustrated. With about 1,000 Original Illustrations. With References, &c. 1,248 pages, crown 4to, cloth, 7s. 6d.

Bible, Cassell's Illustrated Family. With 900 Illustrations. Leather, gilt edges, £2 10s. ; full morocco, £3 10s.

Bible Dictionary, Cassell's. With nearly 600 Illustrations. 7s. 6d. ; roxburgh, 10s. 6d.

Bible Educator, The. Edited by the Very Rev. Dean PLUMPTRE, D.D. With Illustrations, Maps, &c. Four Vols., cloth, 6s. each.

Bible Work at Home and Abroad. Yearly Volume, 3s.

Bible Talks about Bible Pictures. Illustrated by GUSTAVE DORÉ and others. Large 4to, 5s.

Bunyan's Pilgrim's Progress (Cassell's Illustrated). 4to. 7s. 6d.

Bunyan's Pilgrim's Progress. With Illustrations. *Popular Edition*, 3s. 6d.

Child's Life of Christ, The. Complete in One Handsome Volume, with about 200 Original Illustrations. Demy 4to, gilt edges, 21s.

Child's Bible, The. With 200 Illustrations. Demy 4to, 830 pp. 145*th Thousand*. *Cheap Edition*, 7s. 6d.

Commentary, The New Testament, for English Readers. Edited by the Rt. Rev. C. J. ELLICOTT, D.D., Lord Bishop of Gloucester and Bristol. In Three Volumes, 21s. each.
    Vol. I.—The Four Gospels.
    Vol. II.—The Acts, Romans, Corinthians, Galatians.
    Vol. III.—The remaining Books of the New Testament.

Commentary, The Old Testament, for English Readers. Edited by the Rt. Rev. C. J. ELLICOTT, D.D., Lord Bishop of Gloucester and Bristol. Complete in 5 Vols., 21s. each.

Vol. I.—Genesis to Numbers.	Vol. III.—Kings I. to Esther.
Vol. II.—Deuteronomy to Samuel II.	Vol. IV.—Job to Isaiah.
Vol. V.—Jeremiah to Malachi.	

Dictionary of Religion, The. An Encyclopædia of Christian and other Religious Doctrines, Denominations, Sects, Heresies, Ecclesiastical Terms, History, Biography, &c. &c. By the Rev. WILLIAM BENHAM, B.D. Cloth. 21s. ; roxburgh, 25s.

Doré Bible. With 230 Illustrations by GUSTAVE DORÉ. *Original Edition.* Two Vols., cloth, £8 ; best morocco, gilt edges, £15.

Early Days of Christianity, The. By the Ven. Archdeacon FARRAR, D.D., F.R.S.
    LIBRARY EDITION. Two Vols., 24s. ; morocco, £2 2s.
    POPULAR EDITION. Complete in One Volume, cloth, 6s. ; cloth, gilt edges, 7s. 6d. ; Persian morocco, 10s. 6d. ; tree-calf, 15s.

Family Prayer-Book, The. Edited by Rev. Canon GARBETT, M.A., and Rev. S. MARTIN. Extra crown 4to, cloth, 5s. ; morocco, 18s.

Geikie, Cunningham, D.D., Works by :—
    The Holy Land and the Bible. A Book of Scripture Illustrations gathered in Palestine. With Map. Two Vols. 24s.
    Hours with the Bible. Six Vols. 6s. each
    Entering on Life. 3s. 6d.
    The Precious Promises. 2s. 6d.
    The English Reformation. 5s.
    Old Testament Characters. 6s.
    The Life and Words of Christ. Illustrated. Two Vols., cloth, 30s. *Library Edition*, Two Vols., cloth, 30s. *Students' Edition*, Two Vols., 16s. *Cheap Edition*, in One Vol. 7s. 6d.

Glories of the Man of Sorrows, The. Sermons preached at St. James's, Piccadilly. By the Rev. H. G. BONAVIA HUNT, Mus.D., F.R.S.Edin. 2s. 6d.

Gospel of Grace, The. By a LINDESIE. Cloth, 2s. 6d.

Helps to Belief. A Series of Helpful Manuals on the Religious Difficulties of the Day. Edited by the Rev. TEIGNMOUTH SHORE, M.A., Chaplain in Ordinary to the Queen. Cloth, 1s. each.

CREATION. By the Lord Bishop of Carlisle.	THE MORALITY OF THE OLD TESTAMENT. By the Rev. Newman Smyth, D.D.
MIRACLES. By the Rev. Brownlow Maitland, M.A.	
PRAYER. By the Rev. T. Teignmouth Shore, M.A.	THE DIVINITY OF OUR LORD. By the Lord Bishop of Derry.

THE ATONEMENT. By the Lord Bishop of Peterborough.

"Heart Chords." A Series of Works by Eminent Divines. Bound in cloth, red edges, 1s. each.

My Father. By the Right Rev. Ashton Oxenden, late Bishop of Montreal.
My Bible. By the Rt. Rev. W. Boyd Carpenter, Bishop of Ripon.
My Work for God. By the Right Rev. Bishop Cotterill.
My Object in Life. By the Ven. Archdeacon Farrar, D.D.
My Aspirations. By the Rev. G. Matheson, D.D.
My Emotional Life. By the Rev. Preb. Chadwick, D.D.
My Body. By the Rev. Prof. W. G. Blaikie, D.D.

My Soul. By the Rev. P. B. Power, M.A.
My Growth in Divine Life. By the Rev. Prebendary Reynolds, M.A.
My Hereafter. By the Very Rev. Dean Bickersteth.
My Walk with God. By the Very Rev. Dean Montgomery.
My Aids to the Divine Life. By the Very Rev. Dean Boyle.
My Sources of Strength. By the Rev. E. E. Jenkins, M.A., Secretary of the Wesleyan Missionary Society.

Holy Land and the Bible, The. A Book of Scripture Illustrations gathered in Palestine. By the Rev. CUNNINGHAM GEIKIE, D.D. Two Vols., demy 8vo, 1,120 pages, with Map. Price 24s.

"I Must." Short Missionary Bible Readings. By SOPHIA M. NUGENT. Enamelled cover, 6d. ; cloth, gilt edges, 1s.

Life of Christ, The. By the Ven. Archdeacon FARRAR, D.D., F.R.S., Chaplain in Ordinary to the Queen.

ILLUSTRATED EDITION, with about 300 Original Illustrations. Extra crown 4to, cloth, gilt edges, 21s. ; morocco antique, 42s.

LIBRARY EDITION. Two Vols. Cloth, 24s.; morocco, 42s.

POPULAR EDITION, in One Vol. 8vo, cloth, 6s.; cloth, gilt edges, 7s. 6d. ; Persian morocco, gilt edges, 10s. 6d. ; tree-calf, 15s.

Luther, Martin: his Life and Times. By PETER BAYNE, LL.D. Two Vols., demy 8vo, 1,040 pages, cloth, 24s.

Marriage Ring, The. By WILLIAM LANDELS, D.D. Bound in white leatherette, gilt edges, in box, 6s.; French morocco, 8s. 6d.

Moses and Geology; or, The Harmony of the Bible with Science. By the Rev. SAMUEL KINNS, Ph.D., F.R.A.S. Illustrated. *Cheap Edition.* 6s.

Protestantism, The History of. By the Rev. J. A. WYLIE, LL.D. Containing upwards of 600 Original Illustrations. Three Vols., 27s. ; Library Edition, 30s.

Quiver Yearly Volume, The. With 250 high-class Illustrations. 7s. 6d. Also Monthly, 6d.

St. George for England; and other Sermons preached to Children. *Fifth Edition.* By the Rev. T. TEIGNMOUTH SHORE, M.A. 5s.

St. Paul, The Life and Work of. By the Ven. Archdeacon FARRAR, D.D., F.R.S., Chaplain in Ordinary to the Queen.

LIBRARY EDITION. Two Vols., cloth, 24s. ; calf, 42s.

ILLUSTRATED EDITION, complete in One Volume, with about 300 Illustrations, £1 1s. ; morocco, £2 2s.

POPULAR EDITION. One Volume, 8vo, cloth, 6s. ; cloth, gilt edges, 7s. 6d. ; Persian morocco, 10s. 6d. ; tree-calf, 15s.

Secular Life, The Gospel of the. Sermons preached at Oxford. By the Hon. W. H. FREMANTLE, Canon of Canterbury. 5s.

Shall We Know One Another? By the Rt. Rev. J. C. RYLE, D.D., Bishop of Liverpool. *New and Enlarged Edition.* Cloth limp, 1s.

Twilight of Life, The. Words of Counsel and Comfort for the Aged. By JOHN ELLERTON, M.A. 1s. 6d.

Voice of Time, The. By JOHN STROUD. Cloth gilt, 1s.

Educational Works and Students' Manuals.

Alphabet, Cassell's Pictorial. Size, 35 inches by 42½ inches. Mounted on Linen, with rollers. 3s. 6d.

Arithmetics, The Modern School. By GEORGE RICKS, B.Sc. Lond. With Test Cards. (*List on application.*)

Book-Keeping. By THEODORE JONES. FOR SCHOOLS, 2s. ; or cloth, 3s. FOR THE MILLION, 2s. ; or cloth, 3s. Books for Jones's System, Ruled Sets of, 2s.

Chemistry, The Public School. By J. H. ANDERSON, M.A. 2s. 6d.

Commentary, The New Testament. Edited by Bishop ELLICOTT. Handy Volume Edition. Suitable for School and general use.

St. Matthew. 3s. 6d.	Romans. 2s. 6d.	Titus, Philemon, Hebrews,
St. Mark. 3s.	Corinthians I. and II. 3s.	and James. 3s.
St. Luke. 3s. 6d.	Galatians, Ephesians, and	Peter, Jude, and John. 3s.
St. John. 3s. 6d.	Philippians. 3s.	The Revelation. 3s.
The Acts of the Apostles.	Colossians, Thessalonians,	An Introduction to the New
3s. 6d.	and Timothy. 3s.	Testament. 2s. 6d.

Commentary, Old Testament. Edited by Bishop ELLICOTT. Handy Volume Edition. Suitable for School and general use.

Genesis. 3s. 6d.	Leviticus. 3s.	Deuteronomy. 2s. 6d.
Exodus. 3s.	Numbers. 2s. 6d.	

Copy-Books, Cassell's Graduated. Complete in 18 Books. 2d. each.

Copy-Books, The Modern School. Complete in 12 Books. 2d. each.

Drawing Copies, Cassell's "New Standard." Fourteen Books.

Books A to F, for Standards I. to IV.	2d. each.
„ G, H, K, L, M, O, for Standards V. to VII.	3d. each.
„ N, P, ...	4d. each.

Drawing Copies, Cassell's Modern School Freehand. First Grade, 1s. ; Second Grade, 2s.

Electricity, Practical. By Prof. W. E AYRTON. 7s. 6d.

Energy and Motion : A Text-Book of Elementary Mechanics. By WILLIAM PAICE, M.A. Illustrated. 1s. 6d.

English Literature, A First Sketch of, from the Earliest Period to the Present Time. By Prof. HENRY MORLEY. 7s. 6d.

Euclid, Cassell's. Edited by Prof. WALLACE, M.A. 1s.

Euclid, The First Four Books of. In paper, 6d. ; cloth, 9d.

French Reader, Cassell's Public School. By GUILLAUME S. CONRAD. 2s. 6d.

French, Cassell's Lessons in. *New and Revised Edition.* Parts I. and II., each 2s. 6d. ; complete, 4s. 6d. Key, 1s. 6d.

French-English and English-French Dictionary. *Entirely New and Enlarged Edition.* 1,150 pages, 8vo, cloth, 3s. 6d.

Galbraith and Haughton's Scientific Manuals. By the Rev. Prof. GALBRAITH, M.A., and the Rev. P- f. HAUGHTON, M.D., D.C.L.

Arithmetic. 3s. 6d.	Natural Philosophy. 3s. 6d.
Plane Trigonometry. 2s. 6d.	Optics. 2s. 6d.
Euclid. Books I., II., III. 2s. 6d. Books IV.,	Hydrostatics. 3s. 6d.
V., VI. 2s. 6d.	Astronomy. 5s.
Mathematical Tables. 3s. 6d.	Steam Engine. 3s. 6d.
Mechanics. 3s. 6d.	Algebra. Part I., cloth, 2s. 6d. Complete, 7s. 6d.
Tides and Tidal Currents, with Tidal Cards, 3s.	

Geometry, First Elements of Experimental. By PAUL BERT. Fully Illustrated. 1s. 6d.

Geometry, Practical Solid. By Major ROSS, R.E. 2s.

German of To-Day. By Dr. HEINEMANN. 1s. 6d.

German-English and English-German Dictionary. 3s. 5d.

German Reading, First Lessons in. By A. JAGST. Illustrated. 1s.

Handbook of New Code of Regulations. By JOHN F. MOSS. 1s. ; cloth, 2s.

Historical Course for Schools, Cassell's. Illustrated throughout. I.—Stories from English History, 1s. II.—The Simple Outline of English History, 1s. 3d. III.—The Class History of England, 2s. 6d.

Historical Cartoons, Cassell's Coloured. Size 45 in. × 35 in. 2s. each. Mounted on canvas and varnished, with rollers, 5s. each.

Latin-English Dictionary, Cassell's. Thoroughly revised and corrected, and in part re-written by J. R. V. MARCHANT, M.A. 3s. 6d.

Latin-English and English-Latin Dictionary. By J. R. BEARD, D.D., and C. BEARD, B.A. Crown 8vo, 914 pp., 3s. 6d.

Latin Primer, The New. By Prof. J. P. POSTGATE. 2s. 6d.

Laws of Every-Day Life. For the Use of Schools. By H. O. ARNOLD-FORSTER. 1s. 6d.

Lay Texts for the Young, in English and French. By Mrs. RICHARD STRACHEY. 2s. 6d. [1s. 6d.

Little Folks' History of England. By ISA CRAIG-KNOX. With 30 Illustrations.

Making of the Home, The : A Book of Domestic Economy for School and Home Use. By Mrs. SAMUEL A. BARNETT. 1s. 6d.

Marlborough Books.

Arithmetic Examples. 3s.	French Exercises. 3s. 6d.
Arithmetic Rules. 1s. 6d.	French Grammar. 2s. 6d.

German Grammar. 3s. 6d.

Mechanics and Machine Design, Numerical Examples in Practical. By R. G. BLAINE, M.E. With Diagrams. Cloth, 2s. 6d.

Music, An Elementary Manual of. By HENRY LESLIE. 1s.

Popular Educator, Cassell's. *New and Thoroughly Revised Edition.* Illustrated throughout. Complete in Six Vols., 5s. each ; or in Three Vols., half calf, 42s. the set.

Readers, Cassell's "Higher Class":—"The World's Lumber Room," Illustrated, 2s. 6d. ; "Short Studies from Nature," Illustrated, 2s. 6d. ; "The World in Pictures." (Ten in Series.) Cloth, 2s. each.

Readers, Cassell's Readable. Carefully graduated, extremely interesting, and illustrated throughout. *(List on application.)*

Readers, Cassell's Historical. Illustrated throughout, printed on superior paper, and strongly bound in cloth. *(List on application.)*

Readers for Infant Schools, Coloured. Three Books. Each containing 48 pages, including 8 pages in colours. 4d. each.

Reader, The Citizen. By H. O. ARNOLD-FORSTER. With Preface by the late Rt. Hon. W. E. FORSTER, M.P. 1s. 6d.

Readers, The Modern Geographical. Illustrated throughout, and strongly bound in cloth. *(List on application.)*

Readers, The Modern School. Illustrated. *(List on application.)*

Reading and Spelling Book, Cassell's Illustrated. 1s.

School Bank Manual, A. By AGNES LAMBERT. 6d.

Shakspere Reading Book, The. By H. COURTHOPE BOWEN, M.A. Illustrated. 3s. 6d. Also issued in Three Books, 1s. each.

Shakspere's Plays for School Use. 5 Books. Illustrated. 6d. each.

"Slöjd," as a means of Teaching the Essential Elements of Education. By EMILY LORD. 6d.

Spelling, A Complete Manual of. By J. D. MORELL, LL.D. 1s.

Technical Manuals, Cassell's. Illustrated throughout :—

Handrailing and Staircasing. 3s. 6d.	Machinists & Engineers, Drawing for. 4s.6d.
Bricklayers, Drawing for. 3s.	Model Drawing. 3s.
Building Construction. 2s.	Orthographical and Isometrical Projection. 2s.
Cabinet-Makers, Drawing for. 3s.	
Carpenters & Joiners, Drawing for. 3s. 6d.	Practical Perspective. 3s.
Gothic Stonework. 3s.	Stonemasons, Drawing for. 3s.
Linear Drawing & Practical Geometry. 2s.	Applied Mechanics. By Sir R. S. Ball, LL.D. 2s.
Linear Drawing and Projection. The Two Vols. in One, 3s. 6d.	Systematic Drawing and Shading. By Charles Ryan. 2s.
Metal-Plate Workers, Drawing for. 3s.	

Technical Educator, Cassell's. Illustrated throughout. Popular Edition. Four Vols., 5s. each.

Technology, Manuals of. Edited by Prof. AYRTON, F.R.S., and RICHARD WORMELL, D.Sc., M.A. Illustrated throughout.

The Dyeing of Textile Fabrics. By Prof. Hummel. 5s.	Design in Textile Fabrics. By T. R. Ashenhurst. 4s. 6d.
Watch and Clock Making. By D. Glasgow. 4s. 6d.	Practical Mechanics. By Prof. Perry, M.E. 3s. 6d.
Steel and Iron. By Prof. W. H. Greenwood, F.C.S., M.I.C.E., &c. 5s.	Cutting Tools Worked by Hand and Machine. By Prof. Smith. 3s. 6d.
Spinning Woollen and Worsted. By W. S. McLaren, M.P. 4s. 6d.	

A Prospectus on application.

Test Cards, Cassell's Combination. In sets, 1s. each.

Test Cards, Cassell's Modern School. In sets, 1s. each.

A Copy of **Cassell and Company's Complete Catalogue** *will be forwarded post free on application.*

Books for Young People.

"Little Folks" Half-Yearly Volume. With 200 Illustrations, with Pictures in Colour. Boards, 3s. 6d. ; or cloth gilt, 5s.

Bo-Peep. A Book for the Little Ones. With Original Stories and Verses. Illustrated throughout. Yearly Volume. Boards, 2s. 6d. ; cloth gilt, 3s. 6d.

Every-day Heroes. By LAURA LANE. Illustrated. Cloth, 2s. 6d.

Legends for Lionel. New Picture Book by WALTER CRANE. 5s.

Flora's Feast. A Masque of Flowers. Penned and Pictured by WALTER CRANE. With 40 pages in Colours. 5s.

The New Children's Album. Fcap. 4to, 320 pages. Illustrated throughout. 3s. 6d.

The Tales of the Sixty Mandarins. By P. V. RAMASWAMI RAJU. With an Introduction by Prof. HENRY MORLEY. Illustrated. 5s.

Sunday School Reward Books. By Popular Authors. With Four Original Illustrations in each. Cloth gilt, 1s. 6d. each.

Seeking a City.
Rhoda's Reward; or, "If Wishes were Horses."
Jack Marston's Anchor.
Frank's Life-Battle; or, The Three Friends.

Rags and Rainbows: a Story of Thanksgiving.
Uncle William's Charge; or, The Broken Trust.
Pretty Pink's Purpose; or, The Little Street Merchants.

"Golden Mottoes" Series, The. Each Book containing 208 pages, with Four full-page Original Illustrations. Crown 8vo, cloth gilt, 2s. each.

"Nil Desperandum." By the Rev. F. Langbridge, M.A.
"Bear and Forbear." By Sarah Pitt.
"Foremost if I Can." By Helen Atteridge.

"Honour is my Guide." By Jeanie Hering (Mrs. Adams-Acton).
"Aim at a Sure End." By Emily Searchfield.
"He Conquers who Endures." By the Author of "May Cunningham's Trial," &c.

The "Proverbs" Series. Consisting of a New and Original Series of Stories by Popular Authors, founded on and illustrating well-known Proverbs. With Four Illustrations in each Book, printed on a tint. Crown 8vo, 160 pages, cloth, 1s. 6d. each.

Fritters; or, "It's a Long Lane that has no Turning." By Sarah Pitt.
Trixy; or, "Those who Live in Glass Houses shouldn't throw Stones." By Maggie Symington.
The Two Hardcastles; or, "A Friend in Need is a Friend Indeed." By Madeline Bonavia Hunt.

Major Monk's Motto; or, "Look Before you Leap." By the Rev. F. Langbridge.
Tim Thomson's Trial; or, "All is not Gold that Glitters." By George Weatherly.
Ursula's Stumbling-Block; or, "Pride comes before a Fall." By Julia Goddard.
Ruth's Life-Work; or, "No Pains, no Gains." By the Rev. Joseph Johnson.

The "Cross and Crown" Series. Consisting of Stories founded on incidents which occurred during Religious Persecutions of Past Days. With Illustrations in each Book. 2s. 6d. each.

By Fire and Sword: a Story of the Huguenots. By Thomas Archer.
Adam Hepburn's Vow: a Tale of Kirk and Covenant. By Annie S. Swan.
No. XIII; or, The Story of the Lost Vestal. A Tale of Early Christian Days. By Emma Marshall.

Strong to Suffer: A Story of the Jews. By E. Wynne.
Heroes of the Indian Empire; or, Stories of Valour and Victory. By Ernest Foster.
In Letters of Flame: A Story of the Waldenses. By C. L. Mateaux.
Through Trial to Triumph. By Madeline B. Hunt.

The World's Workers. A Series of New and Original Volumes by Popular Authors. With Portraits printed on a tint as Frontispiece. 1s. each.

The Earl of Shaftesbury. By Henry Frith.
Sarah Robinson, Agnes Weston, and Mrs. Meredith. By E. M. Tomkinson.
Thomas A. Edison and Samuel F. B. Morse. By Dr. Denslow and J. Marsh Parker.
Mrs. Somerville and Mary Carpenter. By Phyllis Browne.
General Gordon. By the Rev S. A. Swaine.
Charles Dickens. By his Eldest Daughter.
Sir Titus Salt and George Moore. By J. Burnley.
Florence Nightingale, Catherine Marsh, Frances Ridley Havergal, Mrs. Ranyard ("L. N. R.") By Lizzie Alldridge.

Dr. Guthrie, Father Mathew, Elihu Burritt, Joseph Livesey. By the Rev. J. W. Kirton.
Sir Henry Havelock and Colin Campbell, Lord Clyde. By E. C. Phillips.
Abraham Lincoln. By Ernest Foster.
David Livingstone. By Robert Smiles.
George Muller and Andrew Reed. By E. R. Pitman.
Richard Cobden. By R. Gowing.
Benjamin Franklin. By E. M. Tomkinson.
Handel. By Eliza Clarke.
Turner the Artist. By the Rev. S. A. Swaine.
George and Robert Stephenson. By C. L. Mateaux.

Five Shilling Books for Young People. With Original Illustrations. Cloth gilt, 5s. each.

The Palace Beautiful. By L. T. Meade.
"Follow my Leader;" or, the Boys of Templeton. By Talbot Baines Reed.
For Fortune and Glory; a Story of the Soudan War. By Lewis Hough.
Under Bayard's Banner. By Henry Frith.

The Champion of Odin; or, Viking Life in the Days of Old. By J. Fred. Hodgetts.
Bound by a Spell; or, the Hunted Witch of the Forest. By the Hon. Mrs. Greene.
The King's Command. A Story for Girls. By Maggie Symington.

The Romance of Invention. By Jas. Burnley.

Three and Sixpenny Books for Young People. With Original Illustrations. Cloth gilt, 3s. 6d. each.

The Cost of a Mistake. By Sarah Pitt.
A World of Girls: A Story of a School. By L. T. Meade.
On Board the "Esmeralda;" or, Martin Leigh's Log. By John C. Hutcheson.
Lost among White Africans: A Boy's Adventures on the Upper Congo. By David Ker.

In Quest of Gold; or, Under the Whanga Falls. By Alfred St. Johnston.
For Queen and King; or, the Loyal 'Prentice. By Henry Frith.
Perils Afloat and Brigands Ashore. By Alfred Elwes.
Freedom's Sword: A Story of the Days of Wallace and Bruce. By Annie S. Swan.

The "Boy Pioneer" Series. By EDWARD S. ELLIS. With Four Full-page Illustrations in each Book. Crown 8vo, cloth, 2s. 6d. each.

Ned in the Woods. A Tale of Early Days in the West. | Ned on the River. A Tale of Indian River Warfare.

Ned in the Block House. A Story of Pioneer Life in Kentucky.

The "Log Cabin" Series. By EDWARD S. ELLIS. With Four Full-page Illustrations in each. Crown 8vo, cloth, 2s. 6d. each.

The Lost Trail. | Camp-Fire and Wigwam.

Footprints in the Forest.

The "Great River" Series. (Uniform with the "Log Cabin" Series.) By EDWARD S. ELLIS. Illustrated. Crown 8vo, cloth, bevelled boards, 2s. 6d. each.

Down the Mississippi. | Lost in the Wilds.

Up the Tapajos; or, Adventures in Brazil.

The "Chimes" Series. Each containing 64 pages, with Illustrations on every page, and handsomely bound in cloth, 1s.

Bible Chimes. Contains Bible Verses for Every Day in the Month.
Daily Chimes. Verses from the Poets for Every Day in the Month.

Holy Chimes. Verses for Every Sunday in the Year.
Old World Chimes. Verses from old writers for Every Day in the Month.

Sixpenny Story Books. All Illustrated, and containing Interesting Stories by well-known Writers.

The Smuggler's Cave.
Little Lizzie.
The Boat Club.
Luke Barnicott.

Little Bird.
Little Pickles.
The Elchester College Boys.

My First Cruise.
The Little Peacemaker.
The Delft Jug.

Cassell's Picture Story Books. Each containing 60 pages of Pictures and Stories, &c. 6d. each.

Little Talks.
Bright Stars.
Nursery Toys.
Pet's Posy.
Tiny Tales.

Daisy's Story Book.
Dot's Story Book.
A Nest of Stories.
Good Night Stories.
Chats for Small Chatterers.

Auntie's Stories.
Birdie's Story Book.
Little Chimes.
A Sheaf of Tales.
Dewdrop Stories.

Illustrated Books for the Little Ones. Containing interesting Stories. All Illustrated. 1s. each.

Indoors and Out.
Some Farm Friends.
Those Golden Sands.
Little Mothers and their Children.

Our Pretty Pets.
Our Schoolday Hours.
Creatures Tame.
Creatures Wild.

Up and Down the Garden.
All Sorts of Adventures.
Our Sunday Stories.
Our Holiday Hours.

Shilling Story Books. All Illustrated, and containing Interesting Stories.

Seventeen Cats.
Bunty and the Boys.
The Heir of Elmdale.
The Mystery at Shoncliff School.
Claimed at Last, and Roy's Reward.
Thorns and Tangles.

The Cuckoo in the Robin's John's Mistake. [Nest.
Diamonds in the Sand.
Surly Bob.
The History of Five Little. Pitchers.
The Giant's Cradle.
Shag and Doll.

Aunt Lucia's Locket.
The Magic Mirror.
The Cost of Revenge.
Clever Frank.
Among the Redskins.
The Ferryman of Brill.
Harry Maxwell.
A Banished Monarch.

Cassell's Children's Treasuries. Each Volume contains Stories or Poetry, and is profusely Illustrated. Cloth, 1s. each.

Cock Robin, and other Nursery Rhymes.
The Queen of Hearts.
Old Mother Hubbard.
Tuneful Lays for Merry Days.
Cheerful Songs for Young Folks.
Pretty Poems for Young People.
The Children's Joy.

Pretty Pictures and Pleasant Stories.
Our Picture Book.
Tales for the Little Ones.
My Sunday Book of Pictures.
Sunday Garland of Pictures and Stories.
Sunday Readings for Little Folks.

"Little Folks" Painting Books. With Text, and Outline Illustrations for Water-Colour Painting. 1s. each.

Fruits and Blossoms for "Little Folks" to Paint.

The "Little Folks" Illuminating Book. Pictures to Paint.

The "Little Folks" Proverb Painting Book.

Eighteenpenny Story Books. All Illustrated throughout.

Wee Willie Winkie.
Ups and Downs of a Donkey's Life.
Three Wee Ulster Lassies.
Up the Ladder.
Dick's Hero; and other Stories.
The Chip Boy.
Raggles, Baggles, and the Emperor.
Roses from Thorns.
Faith's Father.

By Land and Sea.
The Young Berringtons.
Jeff and Leff.
Tom Morris's Error.
Worth more than Gold.
"Through Flood—Through Fire;" and other Stories.
The Girl with the Golden Looks.
Stories of the Olden Time.

The "World in Pictures" Series. Illustrated throughout. 2s. 6d. each.

A Ramble Round France.
All the Russias.
Chats about Germany.
The Land of the Pyramids (Egypt).
Peeps into China.

The Eastern Wonderland (Japan).
Glimpses of South America.
Round Africa.
The Land of Temples (India).
The Isles of the Pacific.

Two-Shilling Story Books. All Illustrated.

Stories of the Tower.
Mr. Burke's Nieces.
May Cunningham's Trial.
The Top of the Ladder: How to Reach it.
Little Flotsam.
Madge and her Friends.

The Children of the Court.
A Moonbeam Tangle.
Maid Marjory.
The Four Cats of the Tippertons.
Marion's Two Homes.
Little Folks' Sunday Book.

Two Fourpenny Bits.
Poor Nelly.
Tom Heriot.
Aunt Tabitha's Waifs.
In Mischief Again.
Through Peril to Fortune.
Peggy, and other Tales.

The Magic Flower Pot. | School Girls.

Half-Crown Books.

Little Hinges. .....
Margaret's Enemy.
Pen's Perplexities.
Notable Shipwrecks.
Golden Days.
Wonders of Common Things.
At the South Pole.

Truth will Out.
Pictures of School Life and Boyhood.
The Young Man in the Battle of Life. By the Rev. Dr. Landels.
The True Glory of Woman. By the Rev. Dr. Landels.
The Wise Woman. By George Macdonald.

Soldier and Patriot (George Washington).

Picture Teaching Series. Each book Illustrated throughout. Fcap. 4to, cloth gilt, coloured edges, 2s. 6d. each.

Through Picture-Land.
Picture Teaching for Young and Old.
Picture Natural History.
Scraps of Knowledge for the Little Ones.
Great Lessons from Little Things.

Woodland Romances.
Stories of Girlhood.
Frisk and his Flock.
Pussy Tip-Toes' Family.
The Boy Joiner and Model Maker.
The Children of Holy Scripture.

Library of Wonders. Illustrated Gift-books for Boys. Paper, 1s.; cloth, 1s. 6d.

Wonders of Acoustics.
Wonderful Adventures.
Wonders of Animal Instinct,
Wonders of Architecture.

Wonderful Balloon Ascents.
Wonders of Bodily Strength and Skill.
Wonderful Escapes.
Wonders of Water.

The "Home Chat" Series. All Illustrated throughout. Fcap. 4to. Boards, 3s. 6d. each; cloth, gilt edges, 5s. each.

Home Chat.
Peeps Abroad or Folks at Home.
Decisive Events in History.

Around and About Old England.
Half-Hours with Early Explorers.
Paws and Claws.

Books for the Little Ones. Fully Illustrated.

A Dozen and One; or, The Boys and Girls of Polly's Ring. By Mary D. Brine. Full of Illustrations. 5s.
The Merry-go-Round. Poems for Children. Illustrated throughout. 5s.
Rhymes for the Young Folk. By William Allingham. Beautifully Illustrated. 3s. 6d.
The Little Doings of some Little Folks. By Chatty Cheerful. Illustrated. 5s.
The Sunday Scrap Book. With One Thousand Scripture Pictures. Boards, 5s.; cloth, 7s. 6d.
Daisy Dimple's Scrap Book. Containing about 1,000 Pictures. Boards, 5s.; cloth gilt, 7s. 6d.
The History Scrap Book. With nearly 1,000 Engravings. 5s.; cloth, 7s. 6d.
The Little Folks' Out and About Book. By Chatty Cheerful. Illustrated. 5s.
Myself and my Friends. By Olive Patch. With numerous Illustrations. Crown 4to. 5s.
A Parcel of Children. By Olive Patch. With numerous Illustrations. Crown 4to. 5s.
Little Folks' Picture Album. With 168 Large Pictures. 5s.
Little Folks' Picture Gallery. With 150 Illustrations. 5s.

The Old Fairy Tales. With Original Illustrations. Boards, 1s.; cloth, 1s. 6d.
My Diary. With Twelve Coloured Plates and 366 Woodcuts. 1s.
Happy Little People. By Olive Patch. With Illustrations. 5s.
"Little Folks" Album of Music, The. Illustrated. 3s. 6d.
Cheerful Clatter. Nearly One Hundred Full-page Pictures. 3s. 6d.
Twilight Fancies. Full of charming Pictures. Boards, 2s. 6d.
Happy Go Lucky. 2s.
Daisy Blue Eyes. 2s.
Good Times. 1s. 6d.
Jolly Little Stories. 1s. 6d.
Our Little Friends. 1s. 6d.
Daisy Dell's Stories. 1s. 6d.
Little Toddlers. 1s. 6d.
Wee Little Rhymes. 1s. 6d.
Little One's Welcome. 1s. 6d.
Little Gossips. 1s. 6d.
Ding Dong Bell. 1s. 6d.
The Story of Robin Hood. With Coloured Illustrations. 2s. 6d.
The Pilgrim's Progress. With Coloured Illustrations. 2s. 6d.

Books for Boys.

Commodore Junk. By G. Manville Fenn. 5s.
The Black Arrow. A Tale of the Two Roses. By R. L. Stevenson. 5s.
Dead Man's Rock. A Romance. By Q. 5s.
A Queer Race. By W. Westall. 5s.
Captain Trafalgar. A Story of the Mexican Gulf. By W. Westall. Illustrated. 5s.
Kidnapped. By R. L. Stevenson. Illustrated. 5s.
King Solomon's Mines. By H. Rider Haggard. 5s.
Treasure Island. By R. L. Stevenson. With Full-page Illustrations. 5s.
Ships, Sailors, and the Sea. By R. J. Cornewall-Jones. Illustrated. 5s.

The Phantom City. By W. Westall. 5s.
Famous Sailors of Former Times, History of the Sea Fathers. By Clements Markham. Illustrated. 2s. 6d.
Modern Explorers. By Thomas Frost. Illustrated. 5s.
Wild Adventures in Wild Places. By Dr. Gordon Stables, M.D., R.N. Illustrated. 5s.
Jungle, Peak, and Plain. By Dr. Gordon Stables, R.N. Illustrated. 5s.
O'er Many Lands, on Many Seas. By Gordon Stables, R.N. Illustrated. 5s.
At the South Pole. By W. H. G. Kingston. *New Edition.* Illustrated. 2s. 6d.

Books for all Children.

Cassell's Robinson Crusoe. With 100 striking Illustrations. Cloth, 3s. 6d.; gilt edges, 5s.
Cassell's Swiss Family Robinson. Illustrated. Cloth, 3s. 6d.; gilt edges, 5s.
Sunny Spain: Its People and Places, with Glimpses of its History. By Olive Patch. Illustrated. 5s.
Rambles Round London Town. By C. L. Matéaux. Illustrated. 5s.
Favorite Album of Fun and Fancy, The. Illustrated. 3s. 6d.
Familiar Friends. By Olive Patch. Illustrated. Cloth gilt, 5s.

Odd Folks at Home. By C. L. Matéaux. With nearly 150 Illustrations. 5s.
Field Friends and Forest Foes. By Olive Patch. Profusely Illustrated. 5s.
Silver Wings and Golden Scales. Illustrated. 5s.
Little Folks' Holiday Album. Illustrated. 3s. 6d.
Tiny Houses and their Builders. Illustrated. 5s.
Children of all Nations. Their Homes, their Schools, their Playgrounds. Illustrated. 5s.
Tim Trumble's "Little Mother." By C. L. Matéaux. Illustrated. 5s.

CASSELL & COMPANY, Limited, Ludgate Hill, London, Paris, New York & Melbourne.